The Bomb in the

Bessledorf Bus Depot

Books by Phyllis Reynolds Naylor

The Bomb in the Bessledorf Bus Depot

Phyllis Reynolds Naylor

A Jean Karl Book
Atheneum Books for Young Readers

Atheneum Books for Young Readers
An imprint of Simon & Schuster Children's Publishing Division
1230 Avenue of the Americas
New York, New York 10020

The text of this book is set in Goudy.

FIRST EDITION
Printed in the United States of America
10   9   8   7   6   5   4   3   2   1

Library of Congress Cataloging-in-Publication Data
Naylor, Phyllis Reynolds.
The bomb in the Bessledorf bus depot / Phyllis Reynolds Naylor. — 1st ed.
p.   cm.
"A Jean Karl book."
Summary: After several bombs go off around town, eleven-year-old Bernie
Magruder becomes suspicious of various members of his family, causing
confusion in Officer Feeney's investigation and around the hotel that his
parents run.
ISBN 0-689-80461-X
[1. Mystery and detective stories. 2. Brothers and sisters — Fiction.]
I. Title
PZ7.N24Bn1   1996
[Fic]—dc20
95-30295

For Alexander Holtzman

Contents

One

———

A Little Excitement

The Bessledorf Hotel was on Bessledorf Street be-tween the bus depot and the funeral parlor. Officer Feeney said that some people came into town on one side of the hotel and exited on the other. The Bessledorf had thirty rooms, not counting the apart-ment where Bernie Magruder's family lived, and Feeney said that families gave him more trouble than anyone else.

"Even more trouble than *criminals?*" eleven-year-old Bernie asked as he stood on the corner with the police-man, watching the tourists who came to Middleburg on weekends to shop in the shops, sleep in the hotel, and eat in the hotel dining room where a band played on Saturday and Sunday evenings.

Feeney nodded. "Now you take your average robber,

Bernie. You catch him with his hand in the safe and say, 'Stop or I'll shoot!' and he'll stop still as a stove. But you walk in a house where a husband and wife are fighting and say, 'Stop or I'll shoot!' why, the wife'll hit you over the head with a saucepan, same as she would her husband. She's so mad she can't see straight. I'd a lot rather go after a passel of bank robbers than I would after a wife who's mad at her hubby."

It was a new thought to Bernie—that a simple ordinary family could cause a policeman trouble. Surely not *his* family.

At dinner that night in the apartment of the hotel, where Bernie's father was manager, Bernie ate his peas and silently studied the people around him. His father, Theodore, was talking.

"It has been a good month for the hotel," said Theodore. "Indeed, for the entire town of Middleburg. At the Chamber of Commerce meeting today, it was announced that profits are up in stores all over town. It is the charm of our town that keeps people coming, and we have said 'no' to anyone who wants to change it. We said 'no' to a developer who wants to take away our shops and build high-rises, 'no' to a corporation that wants to turn Middleburg Park into a mall, and 'no' to a fellow who wants to start a bungee-jumping business on the roof of the courthouse."

"I'd *like* to go bungee jumping!" cried Lester, Bernie's younger brother, as he licked the gravy off his fingers.

"I sort of like the idea of a mall," said Delores, the sister, who was twenty years old.

And Bernie's older brother, Joseph, who was a student of the veterinary college, said that more people in high-rises meant more people to bring their pets to the animal clinic. Hence more business for Middleburg.

"My dear, dear family," said Theodore, looking around the table. "There is more to life than excitement, shopping, and making money."

"What?" asked Delores.

"Why, my girl, there is industry, virtue, and courage. There is integrity, perseverance, and truth. Let your mother be an example: seven days a week she works at the registration desk, supervises our dining room, and cooks for our family, yet in her spare time does she sit idle?"

"No," chorused Delores, Joseph, Bernie, and Lester together, as Mother blushed modestly from her end of the table.

"Does she allow her brain cells to rot and her head to go dry?"

"No," chorused the children again.

"Does she allow moth and dust to corrupt where angels fear to tread?"

"No," chorused the children once again.

"No indeed!" repeated Theodore. "When your mother is not working her fingers to the bone, she is writing books."

3

"Which are never published," said Delores, picking up a stalk of celery and chewing loudly.

"Not published *yet!*" said her father. "Rome wasn't built in a day, Delores. Someday your mother will be famous, and *you*, my girl, will be the daughter of a celebrity."

Bernie tried to imagine being the son of a famous author. Everywhere he went, people would ask him the names of the books his mother had written, and Bernie would have to say *Quivering Lips*, *Shivering Shoulders*, and *Trembling Toes*. Maybe he didn't want to be the son of a famous author after all.

"And where would you children be if you didn't have parents who were industrious and persevering?" asked Theodore.

"Blowing about the country like dry leaves in the wind," the children replied in chorus, because they had heard it so often.

"Correct," said their father. "So let us hear no more of shopping, bungee jumping, and making money. Middleburg was meant to be a charming, quiet little town, and that's the way we'll keep it."

As Bernie and Lester lay in bed that night, Bernie on the top bunk, Lester on the bottom, Lester said, "Bernie, remember when we watched people bungee jumping at the state fair? What do you suppose it feels like?"

Bernie thought about it a moment. "I suppose it's like standing in front of a train and knowing you've got only one second to change your mind."

"Well, maybe I wouldn't want to try it, but I'd like to watch *you* do it," said Lester.

"Thank you very much," Bernie told him.

Lester gave a loud sigh, and Bernie heard the crinkle of paper as his brother opened a box of crackers and began eating noisily in the dark. "Nothing exciting ever happens in this town."

"That's not true," Bernie told him. "What about the time we thought there was a mad gasser on the loose? And the time bodies kept appearing and disappearing in the rooms? And when the ghost-boy showed up in Delores's bedroom? What about the time I saw a face in the window of the Bessledorf Funeral Parlor?"

"Yes, but nothing has happened *lately*!" Lester complained. "If we could bungee jump off the roof of the courthouse, then everytime I got bored, all I'd have to do would be to . . . "

BOOM!

An explosion rocked the walls of the Bessledorf Hotel, and Bernie fell right over the side of the bed.

Two

A Hole in the Wall

At first Bernie didn't know whether he had been propelled out of bed or had only fallen out of fright. Lester was still in the bottom bunk, though, so it must have been shock that did it.

"What was *that?*" Lester's voice trembled.

"The excitement you were looking for," Bernie told him, picking himself up.

Outside in the hallway, Mixed Blessing, the Great Dane, began barking frantically. Bernie could hear hurried footsteps in his parents' bedroom, and then the voices of frightened hotel guests as they ran out of their rooms.

The Magruders' apartment was behind the registration desk, and when Bernie and Lester got to the lobby, Delores was there in her pink-flowered kimono, Joseph was in his boxer PJs, and Mr. and Mrs. Magruder had hastily thrown robes over their nightclothes and were trying to quiet Felicity Jones, old Mr. Lamkin, and Mrs. Buzzwell, the regulars who lived in the hotel all the time.

"I was never so frightened in all my life!" gasped Mrs. Buzzwell, in a voice like gravel going down a tin chute.

"Cannons!" cried Mr. Lamkin. "Magruder, I say we're being invaded. Somebody go get my old Springfield, and I'll shoot down the enemy, don't think I won't."

Felicity Jones's wide eyes darted to the left and then to the right. Felicity was a thin young woman who always looked as though she were about to blow away. "Aliens, that's what it sounded like to me," she said. "An alien spaceship landing right on our roof."

By now the switchboard began to light up as other hotel guests called the desk, and Mother tried to reassure them that they were safe.

"My dear friends," Bernie's father said to the crowd that had gathered. "As you can see, we still have our walls and windows, and there is nothing amiss that I can detect. Please calm yourselves and go back to bed. I promise that I shall look into the matter at once, and shall not sleep until I am positive we are all safe. As long as Theodore is awake, you may rest in peace."

"Poor choice of words, Dad," Delores told him.

"Rest assured," Theodore corrected.

By now the street outside was filled with the sound of sirens. The Magruders crowded into the doorway to see what was happening, and Bernie even followed his father outside, PJs or no PJs.

The hotel was still standing, all of it. The roof was still there. Bernie looked up and down the street. The funeral parlor seemed to be all right. Everyone was racing toward the bus depot, however, so he followed his father down the sidewalk, Lester at his heels, Mixed Blessing bringing up the rear.

The depot was still there, too, but Officer Feeney was stringing yellow tape around the front of it so that no one could get through.

"What happened?" asked Bernie.

"Bomb," said Feeney. "Somebody must have placed it in one of the lockers. Blew out a plate-glass window at the back of the depot."

"Was anyone hurt?" asked Father.

"No, but the drinking fountain was blown to bits. The bomb squad's back there right now, investigating." He turned to the crowd again. "Come on, folks, stand back. Let a policeman do his work."

Because the Bessledorf Hotel was right next door, however, Officer Feeney allowed Bernie and his father to make their way through the debris and around to the back, to be sure that the explosion had not ripped a hole in the side of the hotel as well.

There were bricks and dust and glass everywhere. Men from the bomb squad were sifting through the rubble, putting pieces in plastic bags for further analysis.

Bernie was not allowed to pick up anything, of course, but he saw small bits of twisted metal, little strands of rope, charred cloth, chunks of ceramic, and burned wire. How the bomb squad could make anything out of this, he surely didn't know.

At breakfast the next morning, Joseph was sitting at the table over his toast holding a copy of the morning paper. BOMB IN BUS DEPOT, the headline read. Bernie could hardly stand it till Joseph passed the paper to him and he could read it for himself:

> Last night at eleven fourteen, a bomb in a locker at the Bessledorf Bus Depot was detonated, causing considerable damage to the lockers, the back wall, a window, and drinking fountain. There were no injuries. Police theorize that the culprit planted the bomb earlier in the evening, then set it off from a distance. . . .

"Oh, Theodore, who would do such a thing?" cried Mother, delicately spooning the egg from her egg cup. "As though there isn't enough trouble in the world!"

"All manner of people could have done it, my dear," said her husband. "Sometimes it's the person you least expect."

That bothered Bernie. It was sort of like Feeney saying that families gave him the most trouble of all. The people *Bernie* would least suspect of planting a bomb in the bus depot were members of his very own family. But families, as Feeney said, meant trouble.

He looked around the table where Delores was cutting up a banana for her cereal, Lester was licking the jelly off his bread, and Joseph was frowning over his coffee. Father was helping himself to the bacon, and Mother was adding a little sugar to her tea.

Was it possible? he wondered. No, Bernie could not imagine it. No member of his family would ever do such a thing. And yet, *any*thing was possible!

He went to the bathroom to brush his teeth, but when he came back down the hall and passed Delores's room, he saw that she had taken the extension phone in with her.

"*That* fixed him!" Bernie heard her say.

And he got a bad, bad feeling way down in his chest.

Three

___

Peculiarities

That evening Bernie asked his mother: "What's going on with Delores lately?"

"Delores?" asked Mother, as though she'd never heard of her before. Mother was at the registration desk, working on another chapter of *Trembling Toes*, and if you interrupted her when she was working on a book, it took her a while to get away from her characters and back into the bosom of her family.

"Has she been acting odd or anything?" Bernie wondered aloud.

"Now that you mention it, Bernie, your sister has always been a little odd."

"But has she ever . . . done anything really awful? I mean, something I didn't know about?" Bernie asked.

Mother tapped her pencil thoughtfully. "Well, she *did* used to creep up behind your father when he was read-

11

ing and pop a paper bag. She's always loved noise, you know. Loves her music loud. Why are you so interested in your sister all of a sudden?"

"Just wondering," said Bernie, and went on back to his room. For a long time he lay on the top bunk, staring at the ceiling. Was it such a big jump, really, for a girl who loved to make an explosion with a paper bag, to bomb a bus depot?

He went to the telephone and called Georgene Riley and Weasel, his two best friends.

"Come over," he said. "I'm worried."

One of the nicest things about Georgene and Weasel was that they lived so close to the hotel. They could be there in two and a half minutes walking, fifty-five seconds by skateboard. They almost always came by skateboard.

Bernie was waiting for them behind the garden, on the wall next to the alley. Mrs. Verona, the hotel cook, liked to look out the window at her pansies and roses when she was baking, and Bernie enjoyed sitting on the wall and smelling fresh apple strudel or sugar cookies.

In less than a minute he heard the whiz of Georgene and Weasel's skateboards, and Georgene hopped up on the wall beside Bernie, holding her skateboard, the wheels still spinning. Weasel climbed up on the other side of him.

"What?" asked Georgene, holding her ponytail up off

the back of her neck to cool off. She swished it back and forth, fanning her neck.

Bernie took a deep breath. "I think something's really wrong with my sister."

"You're just finding that out, Bernie?" asked Weasel.

"Delores has been wacko since the day I met her," Georgene added.

Bernie wondered if that was true. Delores worked in the parachute factory up on Bessledorf Hill. Maybe a young woman who did nothing but sew straps and pound grommets day after day could not help but be a bit peculiar.

If Delores wasn't falling *in* love with somebody, she was falling *out* of love. If she wasn't telling her mother that she had met the most wonderful man in the world, she was complaining about another. If she wasn't painting her fingernails, she was painting her toenails, and she changed the color of her hair so often that sometimes the only way Bernie knew it was his sister was the fact that she always sat in the same chair at the table.

"Anyway, what's she done now?" asked Weasel, wiping one arm across his freckled face.

Bernie took a second deep breath. "I'm not sure, and I don't have any proof, but . . . promise not to tell anyone?"

His friends nodded.

"She may have bombed the bus depot."

"What?" cried Georgene and Weasel together.

"I know," Bernie said uneasily. "It sounds awful, and I hope I'm wrong, but this morning, after we read about the bomb, I heard Delores talking on the phone in her bedroom. She said, '*That* will fix him.' "

"Fix who?" asked Weasel.

"I don't know, she didn't say."

Georgene and Weasel both stared at Bernie.

"You know, Bernie, *you're* the one who's sounding peculiar," Georgene told him.

"Yeah, I don't see what that has to do with anything," said Weasel.

It was just what Bernie wanted to hear. He even managed a smile. "I guess you're right. It doesn't prove a thing, does it? It was just Delores being weird as usual."

"What *I* heard was that the police are interviewing everyone who was a passenger, or was *going* to be a passenger on a bus last night, to see if there is any connection to the bombing," said Georgene.

"That's smart," Bernie agreed. "A lot smarter than me suspecting my sister."

When the newspaper came the following day, Bernie had just finished breakfast and was sitting at the registration desk with Joseph. As Joseph checked the baseball scores, Bernie looked over the front page.

He saw a list of passengers who were either waiting to get on a bus when the bomb went off or had just come off one. And there was the name of Steven Carmichael,

Delores's old boyfriend, along with his photo. His coat was torn, and there was smoke and plaster dust all over his face. The caption beneath the picture said that Mr. Carmichael had been in the depot to take a bus to Fort Wayne, where he was to meet his fiancée's parents. He had just stepped outside the depot to see if his bus was there when the bomb went off.

Four

A Woman Scorned

"*Look* at him!" cried Delores at dinner, staring at the picture of Steven Carmichael in the paper. "He doesn't look so smart now! He doesn't look so smug!"

"He looks like he got hit by a bomb!" declared Lester.

"Almost but not quite," said Delores. "No such luck."

Bernie looked around the table. Wasn't anybody else upset by this kind of talk?

Father was.

"Delores, my girl," he said. "Where is your Christian charity?"

"Steven *jilted* me, Dad! He promised to love me always, and we were almost engaged to be married when he decided he loved that Fort Wayne floozie instead."

"Now dear," said Mother. "Unless a woman is wearing a man's engagement ring, he is free to lavish his affections on whomever he pleases."

"Lavish-smavish!" said Delores.

"Did you actually pick out a ring?" Joseph wanted to know.

"Not exactly, but I told him that *if* we were to become engaged, I wanted a diamond as large as a pencil eraser with two little rubies on either side."

"Delores!" cried Bernie.

"That does seem rather excessive, my dear," said Mother.

"Well, even though we weren't engaged, he knew that I was ready to be asked, and he had no right to pop the question to that floozie from Fort Wayne," Delores said, sniffing slightly. "What does she have, after all, that I don't?"

"Steven Carmichael?" Lester suggested.

Mr. Magruder cut his pork chop into bite-size pieces and then put down his knife and fork. "Delores, you sound like a woman scorned," he said.

"I *am* scorned!"

"Hell hath no fury like a woman scorned," Theodore went on. "What do you want to do, my girl? String him up by his thumbs and peck out his eyes just because he places his affections elsewhere?"

"He was *trifling* with my affections, Dad."

"Only because the object of his desire lives in Fort Wayne."

"What are they talking about, Bernie?" asked Lester over his applesauce.

"Love," said Bernie.

"Remember this," Theodore went on. "You are a Magruder, Delores. A *Magruder*! Magruders beareth all things, believeth all things, hopeth all things, and endureth."

"I believed Steven Carmichael when he said he loved me, and look what happened!" Delores said tearfully.

"Just the same, we Magruders are a tough lot. Think how close we have come to leaving this hotel, but didn't! Think of all the times we have been only hours away from being back on the street without a morsel of food to sustain us, or a roof over our heads when it snowed. But we always pulled through. Count your blessings, my girl, and remember that behind every cloud is a silver lining, and at the end of every tunnel there is a bluebird."

"For every thorn, there's a rose," said Mother.

"For every pile of manure, there's a horse," said Joseph.

"For every flea, there's a dog," added Bernie.

"For every mud puddle, there's a worm," said Lester.

Bernie thought the conversation would really take off after that, and that his father would ask Delores some tough questions. But the next thing he knew, Mother was passing a carton of ice cream around the table, and everyone was dishing up a scoop or two of maple walnut fudge, and then the meal was over, and he and Lester were on kitchen duty together.

No one had asked Delores if, seeing as how she was delighted that the buses had stopped running two nights ago, she had anything to do with the bomb.

"Delores," he asked his sister, stopping by her room. "When did you first find out that Steven Carmichael was at the bus depot the night the bomb went off?"

His sister looked at him rather strangely. "Why . . . uh . . . a friend called and said that shortly after the bomb exploded, she'd seen Steven walking home, his clothes covered with dust."

Had the friend called Delores to tell her what she'd seen, or had Delores called the friend to tell her what she'd done? Bernie wondered.

"Dad," he said later as he and his father stood at the door of the hotel, looking up at the moon. "When one person goes to prison, does the whole family have to suffer?"

"Indeed they do, my boy. Birds of a feather flock together. If one spoke in a wheel breaks down, the whole tire goes flat."

Bernie felt miserable. "Is it possible that Delores isn't really a member of this family after all?" he asked, hoping against hope.

"Why, my boy, I created her myself. She has my nose and chin. Of course she's mine."

Bernie sighed, and went back into the lobby. But as he stopped at the parrot's cage to cover Salt Water for the night, he realized he had not seen the two cats, Lewis and Clark, since the explosion.

"Dad," he said, running back to his father. "I haven't

19

seen Lewis and Clark since the bomb went off. You don't think that . . . ?"

"I sincerely hope not," said Theodore, and went down to the cellar to check. Soon Bernie had the entire family looking for the cats, and the more he thought about what might have happened to them, the more worried he became.

"We've got to *find* them!" he said to Wilbur Wilkins, the hotel handyman, as he ran back through the lobby again. "If anything happened to Lewis and Clark . . ."

"For heaven's sake, Bernie, they're only *cats*!" declared Delores from the registration desk where she was polishing her nails purple-passion-pink. "Don't get so hyper."

Bernie stopped and stared at his sister. Had she no heart at all? Had she always been this way?

Blinking back tears, he walked right out the door and down the street until he found Officer Feeney walking his beat.

"Mr. Feeney," he said hoarsely, "I think it was my sister who blew up the bus depot."

Five

The Suitor

Almost as soon as the words were out of his mouth, Bernie wished he hadn't said them. Weird as his sister was, she wouldn't do something like that.

Feeney stared down at Bernie.

"Now, Bernie, do you know what you're saying?"

"Probably not," Bernie said in a whisper.

"What do you have for proof?"

"I don't. It was just a thought. Sorry I bothered you," Bernie said, and started to walk away.

"Hold on a minute," said Feeney. "What made you suspect your sister in the first place?"

"It's just the way she's been acting lately, that's all. Her old boyfriend was going to catch a bus that night to meet his fiancée's parents in Fort Wayne, and after the bomb exploded, of course, the bus didn't go. I heard Delores talking to someone on the phone.

'That'll fix him,' she said." Bernie tried to laugh it off.

Officer Feeney smiled a little, too. "Well, now, that doesn't sound good, but it doesn't prove anything either. Just to keep you from worrying about it, though, I'll drop by tomorrow after your sister gets home from work and have a little chat with her. Now you go on to bed and forget it."

Bernie was much relieved to get the matter off his conscience, but he wondered if he should have told his father first before he talked to Feeney. The nice thing was that when he got home, Lewis and Clark emerged from behind the sofa in the lobby where they had hidden after the explosion, and there was general rejoicing that the pets were all accounted for.

The next day Bernie went down to the park with Georgene and Weasel. They skateboarded all around the fountain and sat on the rim in the August sun, their shoes off, dangling their bare feet in the water. Bernie wished he could stay there the rest of the week, because the question that still bothered him was this: If Delores hadn't bombed the bus depot, who had? Would he bomb something else?

The more he thought about it, however, the more he thought how great it would be if *he* caught the bomber. Next to getting his name in the *Guinness Book of World Records* or something, Bernie would love to be a hero and see his name in the newspapers.

That evening, the family had just sat down to dinner

and Theodore had asked the blessing when there was a knock at the back door of the hotel apartment, and Officer Feeney came in.

"Why, Feeney, you just sit right down and have some dinner with us," Mother said. "It's only meatballs and noodles, but you're welcome to it."

"Well, now, I thank you kindly," said Feeney. "It's not often that I get a home-cooked meal. Just stopped by to see what the Magruders are up to these days."

Bernie swallowed and he didn't even have any food in his mouth at the moment.

Everyone scooted over a bit to make room, and Bernie noticed how Feeney kept studying Delores. He swallowed again. This was ridiculous. *Why* had he said anything to Feeney about her?

Feeney sat back as Mother put a big plate of noodles in front of him. "Got to thinking the other day that I'd said hello to all the Magruders lately but Delores, and figured it was about time I ambled over to see how she was doing," he said.

"Now isn't that nice, Delores, that Officer Feeney keeps an eye out for our family?" Mother smiled around the table.

Delores picked up a carrot stick and chewed noisily, one eye on Feeney.

"Have some applesauce, Feeney," said Theodore.

"Don't mind if I do," said the policeman, taking half the contents of the bowl.

"What I'm wonderin', Delores, is what you do with your time when you're not at the parachute factory?" said Feeney.

"You mean when I'm not working my fingers to the bone?" asked Delores. "When I'm not sewing straps until I'm cross-eyed and pounding grommets until my head is like to bust? Do you mean what do I do in the hour or so that a poor working girl can call her own at the end of a hard day in a hostile world?"

"Yeah, I guess that's the hour I'm talkin' about," said Feeney, helping himself to a second pickle. "Maybe you go out with your girlfriends, Delores, or maybe you're sweet on some fella."

"What's it to you, Feeney?" she snapped.

"My girl!" said Father sternly. "Watch your tongue. Just because Officer Feeney asked you a personal question is no reason to raise your feathers and ruffle your hackles."

Delores glared across the table. "Well, I'll tell you this, Feeney. I'm certainly not sweet on Steven Carmichael, may he rot in peace."

"Now, Delores," said her mother.

"Any man who gives you flowers one day and calls a floozy in Fort Wayne the next, deserves to have his pants blown off, and I only regret that Steven Carmichael just got his clothes singed a little."

Bernie closed his eyes. When he opened them, he saw the policeman staring at Delores intently.

"Officer Feeney, I hope you will forgive my daughter, but I'm afraid her heart has been traumatized. She can hardly be held accountable," said Father.

"Oh, no, no, no!" said Feeney. "Please let her continue. It's quite understandable. Let her get it all out. We all need a shoulder to cry on now and then."

Bernie didn't think he could stand it. Delores talked like this all the time, but because of what he had told Officer Feeney, his sister was probably going to jail. He tried to imagine the family getting in the car every Sunday to go visit Delores in the state penitentiary.

It was after Feeney had eaten his second piece of pie and left, and Delores had gone to her room, that Bernie overheard his parents talking together in the kitchen.

"Do you know what I think, Theodore?" Mother was saying. "I think that Officer Feeney has fallen in love with our daughter! Why else would he come to pay a call on her and stay for supper?"

And that was when Bernie thought he really, truly might be sick.

Six

—

Wedding Plans

"I knew it, I knew it, I knew it!"

Mother could hardly contain herself. To a woman who wrote romance novels, a romance under her very nose was even better. "Theodore, it's perfect! It's time that Delores started thinking about a husband, and *past* time for Officer Feeney to be getting married. Both of them are outspoken and somewhat on the grumpy side, wouldn't you say? What they need is each other."

Bernie, listening outside the door, could not see Delores and Officer Feeney married any more than he could imagine himself on Mars.

"Alma, are you quite sure that is why Officer Feeney came by?" asked Bernie's father, sounding skeptical.

"Why else?" said Mother. "*Trust* me, Theodore. I can spot romance at twenty paces. I can hear it, feel it, taste it, smell it, and I tell you, Feeney is enamored of her. He worships the ground she walks on. And why shouldn't he? Our daughter is beautiful, gracious, charming, affectionate, talented, industrious. . . ."

"Delores?" Bernie croaked. He couldn't help himself.

"Bernie, what are you doing outside that door?" Father asked sternly.

"I just happened to be passing by, and thought I heard you talking," Bernie said.

"Well, whatever you heard, I don't want you to repeat it to anyone," Mother told him. "When Delores announces her engagement, I want it to be a surprise." She turned to Father. "We could have the wedding right here in the hotel, Theodore. Just imagine! Our Delores coming down the staircase in a long white dress and veil, with musicians there in the lobby and a buffet in the hotel dining room, with embossed napkins in gold print that say, Delores and . . . uh . . ." Mother stopped. "Theodore, what is Officer Feeney's first name?"

"I don't know, but I'm sure we can find out," said Father.

"I'll ask him," Bernie volunteered.

"Just don't tell him why we want to know," Mother instructed, as Bernie went back outside.

Georgene and Weasel were waiting again with their skateboards, and Bernie herded them back to the alley behind the trash cans. "I'm in a mess!" he said, and explained how he had told Officer Feeney about Delores,

Feeney had come over to question her, and now Mother thought they were in love.

"Don't worry about it," Georgene told him. "When he comes to arrest her, then they'll know the truth."

"I've got to prove it *wasn't* Delores!" Bernie said.

"Good luck!" said Weasel. "If you get any ideas, let us know."

"Well, you guys go skateboarding without me tonight," Bernie said. "I've got to find Feeney."

Officer Feeney was directing traffic around a man who was changing a tire in the intersection. Bernie waited over on the sidewalk. Maybe he would find out that Feeney was already married and had a wife and children down in Texas or something. Maybe he would find out that Feeney didn't want to get married, or was married once and never wanted to marry again.

When the man in the intersection was on his way again, Feeney came over to the sidewalk.

"I was just wondering," Bernie said, "if you have any kids my age."

"Kids? Me?" said Feeney. "Why, Bernie, I'm not even married!"

Bernie sighed, but he didn't give up. "I would think that a dozen women would be after you."

Did he only imagine it, or did the officer blush just a little?

"Now, Bernie, who would want an old flat-footed policeman like me? I ever find a woman who says yes,

I'll marry her soon enough, I'll wager, but so far I haven't got up the nerve to pop the question to anyone."

Oh, no! Bernie thought. If Mother ever found that out, she'd pop the question for him.

"I can't believe that, Feeney," Bernie continued. "With your handsome blue uniform and a name like . . . uh . . .what *is* your full name, Officer Feeney?"

"Hiram Ignatious," the man said softly.

"What?" said Bernie. He couldn't help himself.

"Can you imagine a mother naming her son that?" said Feeney, looking embarrassed. "Hiram Ignatious. After a great-great-uncle or something. Can you believe there's a woman in the world who would want to be married to a man whose name is Hiram Ignatious Feeney?"

No, Bernie could not. He tried to imagine a minister saying, "Do you, Delores, take Hiram to be your lawful wedded husband?" He tried to imagine the wedding napkins with *Delores Jean and Hiram Ignatious* in gold print. He couldn't imagine that either.

"Well, I just wanted to say that I don't think my sister had anything to do with the bombing after all," Bernie said. "I guess I was just sort of upset that night I heard her talking on the phone."

"Maybe you ought to let me decide that," said Feeney. "You did your civic duty, Bernie, and that's what's important."

29

Maybe he should just tell Officer Feeney what was going on, Bernie thought, about his parents suspecting that Feeney was in love. Maybe he should just. . .

BOOMMM!

A second explosion thundered over the town of Middleburg, Indiana.

Seven

Maniac at Large

Bernie stared up into the evening sky. A cloud of smoke and dust was rising slowly up over the roof of the Bessledorf Bus Depot.

"Galloping Galoshes!" cried Feeney. "Not the depot again!"

Bernie broke into a run and followed the policeman down the sidewalk. It *couldn't* have been Delores! Only a short while ago she was there at the table having dinner with the family. And what did *she* know about explosives and how to set them off?

"A maniac, that's who it is!" Feeney said, as he hurried into the waiting room of the bus depot. There was a gaping hole in the wall over by the Coke machine. "Bernie, if your sister's behind this, someone's got to tell Steven Carmichael he'd better fly to Fort Wayne instead."

"She *can't* be!" said Bernie. "Just between us, Officer Feeney, Delores can't even set off an egg timer, much less a bomb. I'm sure I was wrong about that."

"But if anyone has a motive, Bernie, she does. If ever a woman wanted to keep a man from getting on a bus, it's your sister."

Bernie couldn't stand it. "Then just arrest her and get it over with," he said miserably.

Feeney shook his head. "Nope. You can't go around arresting people because of a motive, Bernie. You've got to have more than that. What we need is evidence. Dynamite hidden in the hotel, for example. Now you find me something to make an explosion with, and we'll talk about arresting."

The only thing Bernie knew for sure was that somehow he had to prove that his sister hadn't bombed the depot. Instead of looking for evidence that she had, he had to find evidence she had not. *Could* not. In short, he had to find the bomber.

When he got back to the hotel, *it* was in an uproar. Guests were checking out, afraid to stay in Middleburg any longer but not sure whether they should try to take a bus. Mixed Blessing was barking, Salt Water was squawking, and Lewis and Clark were gone once again.

"Something will be done!" Theodore was saying in a loud voice. "My good people, believe me, we have a top policeman working on this case. As far as we know, the bomber is directing his aggression toward the bus depot, and this hotel is safe. Please calm down, ladies and gentlemen, and stay in the safety of the hotel until the police can complete their investigation."

It didn't help. People were still lining up to check out.

I've got to look for dynamite! Bernie told himself. *If I have to turn this hotel upside down, I'll prove to Feeney that Delores may be flaky, but she's not a nutcake.*

Delores was standing at the front windows with everyone else, watching police cars coming and going, sirens wailing. So Bernie slipped back to her bedroom and began going through her drawers.

Stockings in one. Scarves, sweaters, pajamas. . . .

He looked in her closet. Dresses, pants, skirts, shoes, boots. . . . He looked on the shelves. Hats. An umbrella. Purses. Belts. Sisters, Bernie decided, had the most boring closets in the world.

He looked under the bed. Under the chair. Behind the wastebasket and the small TV. So far so good.

Could there be dynamite hidden in the attic? Just to make sure that Delores didn't go up there every night to make bombs, ridiculous as it seemed, he would check.

Bernie took the elevator to three, then walked up the stairs to the attic. It was gloomy, dark, and dirty. A mouse ran across the toe of his sneaker. A pigeon cooed from the rafters. There were trunks and boxes, old uniforms, lamps, and bedposts. But there was nothing that looked like a bomb. Nothing that smelled like dynamite. Only old photographs of people Bernie didn't even know. Feeney was crazy to have even listened to him.

Okay, what about the basement? It was possible that someone could be making a bomb down there without anyone knowing.

He went downstairs to three. He took the elevator to the lobby, then walked down the narrow staircase to the cellar below and pushed on the old wooden door.

The door wouldn't open. It wouldn't even budge. How could this be? Father never locked the cellar door until he went to bed at night, and always unlocked it first thing the next morning.

Bernie pushed again. He turned the knob this way and that. He knelt down and tried to see through the keyhole. Nothing.

"Looking for something, Bernie?" came a voice behind him, and Bernie wheeled around. There stood Delores at the top of the cellar stairs, looking at him in the oddest way.

Eight

Counting Heads

"What are you *doing*, Bernie?"

Delores demanded an answer.

"I . . . I was looking for Lewis and Clark."

"Well, Mother's frantic and wants to be sure all the family is safe. Come upstairs where she can see you."

Bernie let go of the door handle and came upstairs where his mother had collapsed in a chair. One of the bellhops was fanning Mrs. Magruder's face to revive her.

"Oh, Bernie, my darling, I was so afraid you might have been over there at the bus depot!" Mother cried when she came to, her arms outstretched. She hugged him so hard that she squeezed the breath right out of him, and it took a moment to recover.

"Where's Lester?" she cried suddenly, looking around, and, missing her youngest, immediately fainted again.

More police cars were arriving on the scene, and Bernie could hear Officer Feeney's voice above the din, giving directions and ordering people to stand back.

"No injuries," he heard Feeney yelling to reporters. "Nobody hurt. Please stand back, now, and let the bomb squad through, folks."

"Lester . . . ! Lester . . . !" wailed Mrs. Magruder, as she regained consciousness.

It seemed only a short while ago that Bernie had been trying to imagine what it would be like to visit Delores in prison on Sunday afternoons. Now he found himself imagining Lester in a coffin at the funeral parlor next door. Worse yet, in a coffin in the drive-by window of the funeral parlor next door, so that when Bernie, Georgene, and Weasel walked up the driveway together to pay their respects, music would start to play, lights would come on, the curtains in the drive-by window would open, and there would be Lester, white as a marshmallow, in his Sunday clothes. Bernie would press a button and a drawer would slide out, so that he and Georgene and Weasel could put their names on the registry book.

What do you write in the registry book, when the embalmed is your brother? Bernie wondered.

Bernie Magruder, brother of the deceased, and then what? Perhaps something like *I'll take good care of your baseball cards, Lester.* It was all he could think of.

Now Father was looking worried. "Has anyone seen

our youngest boy?" he asked old Mr. Lamkin who was wandering about the lobby looking very upset and confused. "Felicity? Mrs. Buzzwell? Has anyone seen Lester?"

Bernie realized suddenly that if something happened to Lester, their bedroom would be his alone. Weasel could come over to spend the night and sleep in the bottom bunk—Lester's bunk.

As soon as he had thought it, however, he felt guilty. What kind of boy would think about taking over the bedroom when his brother was gone? The bedroom and Lester's baseball cards as well?

At that moment Mrs. Verona marched into the lobby steering Lester by the collar of his shirt.

"Just waiting for everybody to turn their attention to the bomb, and then he's in my chocolate cake!" she complained, handing Lester over to his father.

Lester had chocolate icing around his mouth and a smear on the front of his T-shirt. "Soon's my back is turned, there he is," she said. "If I didn't know better of the Magruders, I'd suspect he set off that bomb himself just so he could cut himself a slab of my chocolate velvet super fudge supreme layer cake."

Lester? Was it possible? No, Bernie rejected the idea as soon as it entered his head. There were easier ways to distract the cook than setting off a bomb in the bus depot.

"What do you have to say for yourself?" asked Father,

though he didn't sound all that cross. He was too glad to have his youngest son back safe and sound.

"I just couldn't help myself, Dad," Lester told him. "I heard that cake calling, and when I walked in the hotel kitchen, that big four-layer fudge cake just had my name on it."

"Fibs will get you nowhere, my boy," his father said. "Just remember that a lie today means another lie tomorrow and if you make your own bed, you have to lie in it."

"What?" said Lester.

But Mother began to weep out of happiness, and hugged him. "Go wash your hands and face, Lester, and then stay right by me," she said. "I want all four of my children here so I can see for myself they're not dead."

All four? Bernie looked around. There was Delores and Lester and Bernie himself, but where was Joseph?

"Where's Joseph?" asked Mother suddenly.

"Joseph?" called Father. "Has anyone seen Joseph?"

And suddenly Mother began to cry all over again. "Not my oldest son!" she cried. "Oh, no! Not that!"

Now Bernie began to feel very uncomfortable indeed. If Mother felt extra pain at the thought of her youngest son being bombed or her oldest son dead, perhaps she felt that Bernie was expendable, just because he was the middle child. He almost wished that he himself were missing so he could watch outside the window and see what his parents had to say about him.

But a moment later Joseph walked in, and a happier reunion you never saw. Bernie decided he could slip down to the cellar now and prove to Feeney that there was not a trace of explosives anywhere in the hotel.

He went across the lobby and down the narrow stairs to the basement. He put his hand on the door handle, and this time the old wooden door swung open, easy as pie.

Nine

A Little Talk with Feeney

Bernie was relieved. He explored the cellar back and forth, up and down, and found nothing. Absolutely nothing that remotely resembled a bomb. No dynamite. No switches. No gasoline or timers. Mostly the handyman's tools and Joseph's junk, stuff he had lugged home from the veterinary college—old harnesses, cages, ropes, muzzles, splints. Joseph earned a little money part-time repairing things for the veterinary college, and Mother wouldn't let him keep the things in his room. Now Bernie could truthfully tell Officer Feeney that Delores was innocent.

Even if she'd bombed the bus depot the first time to keep Steven Carmichael from going to Fort Wayne to meet the parents of his floozy, why would she bomb it again? The real bomber was out there somewhere, and no one was doing much about it that Bernie could see.

The next day was Saturday, and Bernie got up early.

"What do you think, Feeney?" he said, catching up with the policeman in front of the funeral parlor. "It couldn't be Delores now, could it? I searched the hotel from attic to cellar, and didn't find a thing."

"I was beginning to think it wasn't Delores either," the officer told him, "but we're wrong, Bernie. Dead wrong. Carmichael *did* go to Fort Wayne after all. I checked. Somebody drove him to the airport, and he took the plane. But he was coming back by bus last night. I just found out. So happens, the bus came in early. If it had come fifteen minutes later, it would have been 'Good-bye Stevie,' and a lot of other people, too."

Bernie's heart sank. This was a nightmare that just wouldn't stop.

"All I'm saying," Feeney continued, "is that your sister has the best motive of anyone I can think of. That doesn't make her a *criminal*, mind you, only a suspect. But I'm thinking I ought to have another little talk with Delores."

Oh, no! thought Bernie.

Feeney walked right back to the hotel and went inside.

Georgene and Weasel were coming out of the drugstore across the street, and Bernie motioned them over.

"Feeney's going to have another talk with Delores,

and I want to catch every word," he told them. "I'm *sure* she's not the bomber, and you've got to help me prove it. We'll have to catch the maniac ourselves."

Weasel's eyes opened wide, and Georgene's positively gleamed.

The three slipped inside the lobby and watched while Feeney went straight to the registration desk where Delores was plucking her eyebrows in a little hand-mirror while Mother went over the receipts.

" 'Morning, ladies," Feeney said, half lifting his cap off his balding head and putting it back on again. "Beautiful day out, isn't it?"

"How can you call a day beautiful when there is a maniac loose in our town?" Mother said reproachfully. "We are right next door to that bus depot, Officer Feeney! It could be *us* next! It could have killed Lester if he was over there buying a candy bar. It would have killed Bernie if he were skateboarding through the depot. It could have killed Delores, waiting to meet a girl-friend, or Joseph, gone to see about a sick animal that had wandered in. We entrust our very lives to you, and we want this bombing stopped."

"So do I! So do I!" said Feeney. "The police are doing everything possible to catch the perpetrator, Mrs. Magruder, but we need all the information we can get. I wonder . . . long as I'm here . . . if I might have another little talk with Delores."

Bernie saw his sister roll her eyes, but Mother looked positively delighted.

"Of course, Officer Feeney! Why don't you two go right back in the apartment. There's a loveseat right by the window, and you can talk in private."

"Oh, that won't be necessary, ma'am," Feeney said. "We can sit right over there on the couch in the lobby."

"Quick," Bernie said to his friends. "It's time to clean out Salt Water's cage."

So while Delores disgustedly put down her mirror and tweezers, and came out from behind the registration desk, Bernie and his friends quietly set about changing the paper at the bottom of the cage there in the lobby, brushing out the seeds, adding more, bringing fresh water, their ears perked for every word they could hear from the couch.

"*Now* what, Feeney?" Delores said crossly, plunking herself down at one end of the sofa, Feeney at the other. Delores was chewing gum, and she somehow made it crackle with every chew.

"Oh, just want to see what's new with you," Feeney said. "Wondered if you've talked to that Carmichael chap lately."

"Carmichael *cheat* is more like it. It'll be a warm day in January before I have anything to say to him!" Delores declared.

"Well, now, Delores, I'm wondering if you didn't

43

know that Steven was going to get to Fort Wayne one way or another. Just so happens, he flew to Fort Wayne and came back on a bus last night, just fifteen minutes before the second bomb went off."

Delores's eyes opened wide. "He went to Fort Wayne after all? He saw that floozy's parents and probably asked for their daughter's h . . . hand in m . . . marriage?" Suddenly Delores's eyes closed and her mouth opened wide in a loud wail. "Waaaah! It could have been *my* hand! It could have been *my* parents! It could have been *me* in a long white dress and veil!"

Bernie, Georgene, and Weasel stopped cleaning the parrot's cage and stared, but Officer Feeney was caught off guard.

"Now, now, Delores, don't take it so hard," he said, and gingerly put his arm around her shoulder. "Just tell old Feeney all about it. A little confession is good for the soul, you know."

"I . . . I *loved* him!" Delores cried. "I *trusted* him! I thought I'd be Mrs. Steven Carmichael by C . . . Christmas! Oh, that rotten louse! I could break every bone in his body!"

And when Bernie went over to the registration desk to get more newspaper for Salt Water's cage, he heard his mother whisper to Theodore, who had just come in, "What do you think about the wedding cake, Theodore? Do you think Feeney would like white or lemon?"

Ten

The Test

"I don't think Delores did it," said Georgene when the three friends took Mixed Blessing for a walk later. "I don't think she was crying false tears. I honestly believe she *didn't* know that Steven Carmichael was coming back by bus when the second bomb went off."

"So do I," said Bernie, even though a woman scorned, according to Father, was capable of almost anything. "But how are we going to prove it, unless we find the bomber ourselves?"

"I know how we can prove it," said Weasel.

Bernie and Georgene turned and looked at him. "How?" they asked together.

"A little test," said Weasel, looking very mysterious. "Bernie, how smart is your sister, on a scale of one to ten, ten being the highest?"

"Maybe a two," said Bernie.

"That's what I thought. Okay. Follow me." Weasel started down the alley, Georgene and Bernie following curiously along behind.

What would he ever do without friends? Bernie wondered. Georgene and Weasel were always there for him when he needed them.

When they reached the side street, they walked to the corner, then crossed to the library where Weasel climbed up the steps and reached for the low branch of a tree. He broke off a small twig with two yellow leaves on it.

"Look," he said, holding it out for Bernie and Georgene to see. "Look at that dark stuff at the base of each leaf. I noticed it the other day."

"So?" said Bernie. "What does this have to do with Delores? Will she know what it is?"

"*I* don't even know what it is," said Weasel. "But if you're sure Delores won't, we're in business."

"Delores won't even know what kind of a tree it's from," said Bernie. "Trust me."

"But what are you going to do?" asked Georgene.

"You'll see," Weasel told her.

When they got back to the hotel, Bernie led them into the hotel apartment where Delores had just taken a shower. She came out of the bathroom in her robe with a towel wrapped around her hair.

"Look what we found," said Weasel, and held up the yellow leaf with the sticky sap at the end.

"It's a leaf," said Delores. "So what?" And went on down the hall toward her bedroom.

"But did you see what was on the end of it?" asked Weasel.

"Something gross. Some kind of sap or something," Delores said, and sat down on her bed to cut her toenails.

"It's a special kind of sap," Weasel told her. "It's poison."

"Poison?" Delores put down the scissors and stared at the twig.

Weasel nodded and his glasses slipped down a little farther on his nose. "One little drop of this in somebody's coffee and he wouldn't even notice. But about five minutes later—bonk! Over he goes. We learned it in science. Never lick the leaves of the spudgrass tree."

Spudgrass? Bernie wondered.

"Just like that?" Delores asked.

Weasel nodded again. "That's all there is to it. Just put a drop in somebody's coffee, he drinks it, and he's gone. Nobody would ever know what happened."

Delores's eyes grew wide. She held out her hand. "Give it to me?" she begged.

Bernie's heart dropped to his knees. She was going to do it! She was going to do Steven Carmichael in! If she didn't get to prison one way, she'd get there another. Bernie had been right about his sister in the first place, and Feeney knew it.

He and Georgene watched breathlessly as Weasel placed the twig in Delores's open palm.

As soon as her fingers closed over the two leaves, she got up and walked back to the bathroom. And as Bernie, Georgene, and Weasel stared, she flushed it down the toilet.

"You kids shouldn't be playing with something as dangerous as that," she said. "Go ride your skateboards or something."

Bernie let out his breath in relief. Maybe Delores was smarter than he thought! Maybe she was a three or even a four!

"Well," said Weasel, when they got outside. "She passed the test. If she had murder in mind, she would have kept that leaf and used it on Carmichael. She's not the bomber."

"Then we've got to find out who is, because Feeney suspects her," said Bernie.

"*Think*! Who would be mad enough at a bus depot to want to bomb it?" said Georgene.

"One of the drivers, maybe?" Bernie suggested. "One of the drivers got fired, maybe, and he's trying to get back at the company?"

"Could be any employee at all. A ticket agent. A janitor," said Weasel.

Georgene sprawled on the back steps. "What about customers? What about people who *ride* the bus? Maybe a bus was late just once too often, and a customer missed something important and wanted to get even."

Bernie stared at his friends. *Steven Carmichael?* Was it possible that instead of being all covered with dust because someone had tried to bomb *him*, he was dusty because *he* set off the bomb?

"Steven Carmichael?" he said aloud.

"Delores's old boyfriend? *Why?*" asked Weasel.

Bernie shrugged. "I don't know, but he was there at the depot both times. Maybe he just wanted to look like one of the victims."

"But what's so awful in Middleburg he'd want to bomb it?" asked Georgene.

"My sister," said Bernie.

"You just might be right," said Weasel. "Let me think about this awhile. Maybe I'll come up with something."

When Bernie went in later for dinner, he decided he needed to talk this over with somebody—someone he could trust. Joseph, maybe! Just a brother-to-brother talk.

As soon as the meal was over, Bernie followed Joseph into the bathroom where they both brushed their teeth. Bernie brushed and rinsed and flossed and rinsed again, but when he turned around to talk to Joseph, his brother was gone.

Eleven

A New Suspect

Of all his siblings, Bernie liked Joseph best. Joseph was not a complainer like Delores, and he wasn't always doing something gross, like Lester. If it weren't for Joseph, in fact, the Magruders would not have the wonderful pets he had brought home; and if there was ever a kind word to be said, Joseph was the one to say it.

Of all his siblings, however, Bernie probably saw the least of Joseph, because his older brother always seemed to be studying. If he was not studying for a test on invertebrate animals, he was doing an assignment on diseases of goldfish. If he was not writing a paper on ear mites in housecats, he was reading up on the digestive tracts of dogs. He regularly brought his textbook to the dinner table, and read about swine fungus or udder problems in Holsteins.

"Why couldn't you do something useful with your life, like studying the hair problems of American women?" Delores asked him at dinner. "Or nail problems among the female population of Indiana?"

"Delores, my girl," her father said, "there are bigger problems to think about in this world than yours. Of all the problems going on in Middleburg at this moment, yours hardly amount to the lint in your belly button."

"What other problems, dear, besides the bombing of the bus depot?" Mother asked.

"Everywhere you look there are problems," Theodore said wearily. "There was another meeting of the Chamber of Commerce today. The developer who wanted to build high-rises said he could solve the bus depot problem by simply tearing it down and building a high-rise there. The corporation that wanted to build a mall said they could use the first floor of the high-rise for a minimall, and the man who wanted to start a bungee-jumping business on the roof of the courthouse said that people could jump off the roof of the high-rise instead."

Lester clapped his hands delightedly, but Theodore gave him a stern look.

"But if Middleburg has high-rise buildings and malls and bungee jumping, it won't be the little town we know and love," said Mother. "And how is anybody supposed to get here if we don't have a bus depot?"

"Exactly!" said Father. "That's what I told them at the meeting, but they suggested we build a bus depot somewhere else."

"If someone has a grudge against the bus depot, they'll bomb it no matter where it is!" said Bernie.

"Bernie, my boy, you have a lot more sense than our mayor," Father agreed. "That's what I told them. If there is a maniac who has a grudge against our bus depot, he'll bomb it, torch it, flood it, gut it no matter *where* we build it. The one thing you can't hide is a bus depot. I finally made them see the light of day, but it was an effort, believe me."

"My poor darling," said Mother.

It was time, Bernie decided, that he and Joseph had a heart-to-heart talk about Delores, Steven Carmichael, and who was and who was not a suspect in the bus depot bombing.

Bernie looked in Joseph's room, but his brother wasn't there. He went out in the garden, where Joseph sometimes took Mixed Blessing to brush the dog's coat, but his brother wasn't there either. Maybe he went back to the veterinary college to feed the animals, Bernie thought.

He went inside to the registration desk where Mother was having a conversation with Hildegarde, the cleaning woman, about bedsheets.

"Have you seen Joseph?" Bernie asked the red-haired cleaning woman, whose skin was as pasty as the inside of a potato.

"Saw him not more than ten minutes ago, a big bag under his arm," the cleaning woman said.

Bernie looked down the hall where Wilbur Wilkins, the handyman, was changing a lightbulb.

"Have you seen Joseph?" he asked.

"Think I saw him heading down to the cellar," Wilbur said.

Bernie went down the narrow stairs to the wooden door at the bottom. But when he pushed on the heavy door, he found it locked.

He knocked on the door. "Joseph? You there?"

No answer. Bernie put his ear to the door and listened. No sound.

"Joseph?" he called again, louder. "Hey, Joseph, I want to talk to you."

Still no answer.

Now Bernie was really worried. Father locked the door at night after the cats had been let out, so no robber could crawl in through a basement window and come up into the apartment. But he unlocked the door every morning when the cats came in, and always left it ajar so they could use their litter box when necessary.

Bernie went to find his father.

"Dad, I think something's going on in our cellar," he said.

"What do you mean, 'going on'?" his father asked. "A card game or a murder?"

"Something strange," said Bernie. "I've been looking

all over for Joseph, and Wilbur Wilkins saw him heading for the cellar. But the door down there is locked."

"Why, I unlocked that door this morning," said Father. "I'll take my key and see what's what."

As they started down the cellar steps, however, they met Joseph coming up.

"Why didn't you let me in?" Bernie asked. "I knocked and knocked."

"You did?" asked Joseph. "Just push harder next time, Bernie, and the door will probably open."

"A little more muscle power," said Father, smiling at Bernie.

Theodore turned and went back upstairs, and Joseph followed. Bernie tried not to think what he was thinking, but the thoughts came anyway. He went to the cellar to check again. He could see nothing that shouldn't be there, however—no dynamite, no fuses, no matches, no bombs.

He struggled to figure it out. Joseph had been doing *some*thing secret here in the basement, or he wouldn't have locked the door. But if *he* was making bombs, why? Delores, as far as he could tell, wasn't making bombs at all, but she certainly would have liked to.

Then Bernie had another idea. It was such an awful thought, a sickening thought, that his legs felt wobbly and he had to sit down. If Joseph had been making a bomb but had no reason to blow anyone up, and

Delores had a reason but didn't know how, perhaps Delores was paying Joseph to make the bombs *for* her!

No! he told himself. Somebody else had bombed the Bessledorf Bus Depot, and he would find out who.

Twelve

Phone Call from Indianapolis

According to the *Bugle*, a maniac had taken up residence in Middleburg, and no telling where he'd strike next.

Delores was indignant when she read the paper. So was Mother.

"Why is it always a *man* that anyone thinks of as having enough cunning and smarts to set off a bomb?" Delores fumed.

"Women have passions, too!" declared Mother. "Don't those stuffed shirts at the newspaper think that a woman could be capable of an act of great drama?"

Theodore had a coughing fit at his end of the table, and finally he stood up, waving his arms, while Joseph pounded him on the back. When he was in control of himself again, he said: "Ladies! Ladies! I am shocked, astounded, flabbergasted, and amazed. That the women in my house would express such emotions! Where is the hand that rocked the cradle? The voice that stilled the babe? The tender smile, the rosy lips, the silver hair, the . . ."

"Can it, Dad," said Delores. "This is the 1990s, and we have as much right to anger and indignation as anyone else. Steven Carmichael deserves whatever happens to him."

"Delores," said Father sternly. "Go to your room. And Alma, if you cannot set a better example for a daughter than this, you should hang your head in shame."

Bernie had never heard his father talk to his mother like this before. He couldn't imagine his mother hanging her head in shame for anybody, and if Delores went to her room, she wouldn't have to do the dishes that night. *He* would.

Now Mother stood up.

"Theodore, I have a good notion to put you in one of my books," she said. "You could be Penelope Pennyworth's unfeeling father, a man who believes that women should only work in the house, and if there is any action to be taken, the men will do it."

Father stared. Mother had never threatened to put him in a book before. This was serious!

"See?" cried Bernie, genuinely alarmed. "See what's happening to our family because of the bombs?"

Just then the telephone rang, and as Bernie was closest to it, he answered.

"Hello?" he said. The next voice he heard was that of the hotel owner, Mr. Fairchild, from Indianapolis, so he handed the phone to his father.

"Theodore?" Mr. Fairchild boomed when Father answered. His voice could be heard all over the room. "I've been hearing about those bombs going off in Middleburg, and I want every person checked for explosives before he enters my hotel."

Bernie went outside to think. If the hotel was bombed next, this could change everything. Then it would *prove* that Delores and Joseph weren't setting off bombs, because they wouldn't bomb their own home!

He went searching for Officer Feeney. The policeman was having a cup of coffee at the drugstore.

Bernie slid onto a stool beside him.

"Now, Bernie," Feeney said, "if you think that by sliding up to me at this counter I'm going to order you a chocolate fudge sundae with a cherry on top, you've got the wrong man."

Bernie hadn't even given a thought to fudge sundaes until Feeney suggested it, but now his mouth said it would like the taste of creamy fudge on his tongue more than anything else he could think of.

"What would you say if I told you I have a hot tip about where the next bomb is going to go off?" Bernie said.

"The *next* bomb? You mean there'll be more? I'd say one hot fudge sundae coming up, extra cherries, double cream," said Feeney. And when it was set before Bernie, the policeman looked at him and said, "Well?"

Bernie took a bite first before he answered. "We got a phone call a little while ago from Mr. Fairchild in Indianapolis. He said he's afraid the next bomb is going to go off somewhere in our hotel." Well, that was *sort* of what Mr. Fairchild said, wasn't it?

"The Bessledorf?" Feeney said, his eyes wide. "A bomb going off in your hotel, and you're sitting here calm as a cake of soap?"

"I guess I'm relieved that it's not anybody in my family after all who's been making those bombs."

"And just how do you figure that?" asked Feeney.

"Why would anybody set off a bomb in his own home?"

"Why, Bernie, that's exactly where they *would* set it off. To throw the police off their trail, that's why."

Bernie's heart sank once again, and he wasn't sure whether to finish the fudge sundae or not.

"What I want to know is where does Fairchild get his tips? Maybe Fairchild's got something to do with the bombing," said the policeman. "Wouldn't be the first time the owner of an old hotel blew it sky high just to collect the insurance money."

Oh boy, now Bernie was in over his head. He wished he'd never said anything about Mr. Fairchild. He wished he'd never said anything about Delores. He stared at his chocolate fudge sundae, but didn't feel much like eating it.

Thirteen

A Nose for Trouble

Bernie, Georgene, and Weasel sat in a row on the couch in the lobby and watched people come in and out.

"How can you tell which one is a bomber?" said Weasel. "Go look in everyone's pockets? Search all the rooms?"

"I vote for Fairchild," said Georgene. "I've heard that if somebody owns a building that isn't making much money and costs too much to keep up, he burns it down and claims it was an arsonist."

"But that's *criminal!*" Bernie exclaimed.

"Of course, but maybe Fairchild thinks he can get away with it. First he bombs the bus depot a couple times and then he bombs the hotel. If he bombed the hotel right off, the police might suspect him, but if bombs are going off other places, too, no one would think of him. And if the bomb destroys enough of the hotel, the insurance company will pay to have it demolished and send a big fat check to Fairchild."

Life seemed to be getting worse and worse for Bernie Magruder. Whom could he trust? How did he know the bomb wouldn't go off and kill his entire family?

But then he got a marvelous idea. "Why don't we teach Mixed Blessing to sniff out explosives?" he said.

"Good idea, Bernie, but slightly stupid," said Georgene. "Where do we get some dynamite?"

"It doesn't have to be dynamite, does it?" Bernie questioned. "All you need is a little gunpowder. Cap guns, caps, fireworks, sparklers . . ."

"I don't have a cap gun," said Georgene.

"I don't have any sparklers," said Weasel.

"Let's check out Lester's drawers," Bernie told them, and led his friends to the room he shared with his younger brother. The only problem was that Lester was in it.

"Lester, could we borrow your cap gun?" Bernie asked.

Lester was reading a comic book on the bottom bunk and eating a banana stuck full of stick pretzels. It looked like a porcupine banana. Everytime Lester took a bite, it made a crunching sound.

"It'll cost you," he said.

"How much?"

"Hershey bar, no almonds."

"Okay. Any caps in the gun?"

"Those'll cost you, too. Milk Duds, large size."

"I'll spring for those," said Weasel.

"How about fireworks—sparklers, fizzies, sizzlers—anything?" asked Georgene. She leaned over the bunk and looked into Lester's eyes. "*Please*, Lester? Pretty please?"

"Okay. In my dresser, third drawer down," Lester said.

The three friends took the stuff they had borrowed from Lester and went back into the lobby for Mixed Blessing. Instantly the Great Dane was up on his feet and began licking Bernie, Georgene, and Weasel up one side of their faces and down the other.

They all went outside to the alley.

Bernie took a rock and pounded the roll of caps until a few of them popped, and there was the smell of gunpowder in the air. He rubbed the used caps on his hands.

"Smell, M.B.," he said to the big dog. "Take a big sniff."

The dog sniffed at Bernie's hands—over, under, and between each finger.

"Now walk him down to the end of the alley and come back," Bernie told his friends.

When they were gone, Bernie took the lids off seven garbage cans and set them in a row in the alley. Under one of the lids he put the caps. Under another he put the cap gun. Under still another, farther down, he put the sparklers and sizzlers.

Georgene and Weasel came back with Mixed Blessing.

Bernie let the dog sniff his hands again and then he pointed to the seven trash can lids.

"Find!" Bernie commanded. "Go *find*, M.B."

Mixed Blessing wagged his tail.

Bernie let the dog smell his hands again. "Go find!" he said, even more sternly than before.

The dog walked around behind Bernie and smelled his hands from behind.

"Go *find*, you flea-brained bag of bones!" Georgene said crossly.

Mixed Blessing went down the alley, nosing under each garbage can lid. He found the cap gun, then the caps, then the fireworks, and kept going until every trash can lid had been turned upside down.

"Now what do we do?" asked Weasel. "We don't know if he kept on looking because he didn't know he'd already found the stuff, or because he thought there might be more. How do we even know he could smell it at all?"

"We'd better talk to Feeney," said Bernie, and they went in search of the policeman. When they found him, Bernie explained about training the dog to sniff out bombs.

"Now that's a fine idea if I ever heard one," Feeney said. "Bring him on over to the police station, and we'll give him a course in sniffing."

At the police station, Bernie, Georgene, and Weasel sat on a bench outside while Officer Feeney took the dog back to the lab.

"How do you suppose they know when he's ready?" Georgene asked. "Another test?"

"Multiple choice," said Weasel.

"No, true or false," said Bernie. "One bark for yes, two for no."

After a long time, Officer Feeney came out with Mixed Blessing on a leash.

"Did he pass?" asked Bernie.

"Top of his class," said Feeney. "Watch." He led the children into the training area. At the far end there were five colored boxes, each five feet apart.

"We've been moving the dynamite around from box to box. Your dog doesn't know which one it's under, but he can find it," Feeney told them. He looked down at Mixed Blessing. "Fetch!" he commanded, letting go of the leash.

Mixed Blessing went trotting over, tongue hanging out. He made a quick pass at the yellow box, then the green one, and when he came back to the blue box, he immediately began to bark.

"Good work!" said Officer Feeney. He went to the end of the room and lifted the blue box. There underneath was the dynamite. Feeney patted the dog on the head. "Take him home, Bernie, and let him sniff out the guest rooms. That will tell you who's planning to do you in, I'll wager. If you find anything suspicious, give us a call."

Bernie proudly walked Mixed Blessing back up the street. He wasn't walking just any old dog; he was walking a certified dynamite sniffer.

In the hotel kitchen, Mother was giving Hildegarde and Wilbur Wilkins a lecture.

"I want you to report *any*thing at all unusual that you see until the maniac bomber has been caught," she said. "We're afraid he might strike the hotel."

Hildegarde clutched at her throat and her face looked even more like a potato. It looked, in fact, like clotted cream. "I don't care how much you pay me, Mrs. Magruder, I'm not sticking around to get my head blown off," she said.

"Me either," said Wilbur Wilkins, putting down his hammer. "I've put up with a lot in this hotel, ma'am, but I draw the line at a maniac bomber."

"Wait!" said Bernie. "I've got the answer! Mixed Blessing has just been through an explosives-detection course at the police station, and he can sniff out dynamite like nobody's business." And he showed them the dog's certificate.

"We'll take him through all the rooms," Mother said, much relieved. "If anybody here has explosives hidden away, we'll soon find them."

"But who's to say that the maniac bomber is staying in this hotel?" asked Hildegarde. "He could walk in some day with dynamite in his toolbox and say he's a plumber. How would we know?"

"Then we will have every person who enters our hotel go past Mixed Blessing for a sniff test," Mother declared. "If he doesn't pass, we'll call Officer Feeney."

When Father heard the news, he said they would sleep better at night, knowing that Mixed Blessing was around.

Unless, Bernie told himself, the maniac bomber was Delores or Joseph, who took the dynamite *out* of the house when Mixed Blessing made his rounds, and brought it in again when the dog was through. He wished that Feeney had never said what he did about how families gave him the most trouble. Bernie might never have thought of Delores or Joseph as suspects if Feeney had just kept his ideas to himself.

Fourteen

The Sniff Test

Theodore stationed Wilbur Wilkins with Mixed Blessing inside the front entrance of the Bessledorf Hotel, and everyone who came in had to stop first for inspection.

"I was never so humiliated in my life!" cried Mrs. Buzzwell. "To be sniffed at like an animal—by an animal—is almost more than human dignity can bear."

"What you will lose in dignity you will gain in personal safety," Theodore told her. "It is a small price to pay for knowing that you will not be blown out of your bed in the middle of the night."

"Or straight up out of the bathtub naked," added Lester.

"What you ought to do, Magruder, is have a cannon in the doorway of the Bessledorf, and if Mixed Blessing finds the bomber, fire away!" said old Mr. Lamkin.

"Every man is innocent until proven guilty, sir," Father told him, "even those with dynamite in their pockets and their hands in the cookie jar."

"A better test," said Felicity Jones in her wispy voice, her thin lips barely moving in her pale face, "is to look deep within the person's eyes. There will be a certain aura about the pupils of a bomber, a certain haze above the eyelid, a certain scent, a certain . . ."

"Well, you just gaze away, Felicity, while Mixed Blessing does his sniffing," Father told her. "To each his own, it takes all kinds to make a world, and don't fire till you see the whites of their eyes."

So all day long, people entering or leaving the Bessledorf Hotel stopped by the little desk where Wilbur Wilkins was stationed with the Great Dane, and after their pockets and purses and shoes and trousers had been sniffed, they were allowed to go on their way. After a few days, even Mrs. Buzzwell had to admit that she was sleeping better.

Then a man whom Bernie had never seen before came to town. This was not at all unusual, for many people came to Middleburg to shop the shops and eat the eats and swim the lake and tour the courthouse.

But the strange thing about the man in room 203 was that he carried a large leather bag with him. Not a suitcase, but a bag. Just before he entered the hotel, Wilbur Wilkins had taken Mixed Blessing back to the alley to do his business, and by the time they got back, Mr. Edgar Sutton had been checked in and was already on the elevator going up to the second floor.

"What could I do, Theodore?" asked Mother. "Tell a perfect stranger he had to wait until the dog came back to sniff him?"

"It's worked so far, Alma," Father told her. "No one else has objected."

"Well, perhaps when he comes down to dinner we can test him then," Mother said.

"By dinner, my dear, we could all be dead! Who knows what he is carrying in that valise!"

"Maybe we could take Mixed Blessing up to his room right now and check him out," suggested Bernie.

"A man's room is his private domain, Bernie," Father reminded him. "We never intrude upon the privacy of our guests unless it's a matter of life or death."

"Then we'll all die!" said Delores, who had just come home from the parachute factory and heard the conversation. "It *is* a matter of life or death."

"All right, my dears, here's what we'll do," Father told them. "If the man leaves the hotel for any reason between now and dinner, we will go to his room and check it out. Otherwise, we will wait until he comes to the dining room and check him then."

Everyone waited as the clock ticked on. Bernie didn't think he could stand it. At every slam of a door or beep of a horn, the family jumped. Every time the elevator doors opened, all eyes looked in that direction to see if the man from 203 was getting off.

Finally Father himself could stand it no longer, and dialed Mr. Sutton's room number.

"Hello, Mr. Sutton," he said. "I just wanted to welcome you to the dining room of the Bessledorf Hotel, should you care to have dinner with us tonight, and to remind you that dinner at the Bessledorf is a gourmet's delight. Tonight, for example, we are having cream of escargot soup, fillet of sole almandine, steamship round of beef with asparagus tips, potatoes Florentine, and a white mousse for dessert."

"A white moose?" cried Lester. "Who shot it?"

"Hush," said Mother.

"You will, sir?" Father was saying. "Very good, sir. We will hold your reservation for seven o'clock."

After Theodore hung up the phone he said in a whisper, "He's coming!"

The family waited again, all eyes on the elevator. When the door opened, there stood the man from 203, holding the leather bag to his chest, just as he had when he checked into the hotel.

Instantly, Mixed Blessing sat up and sniffed the air. As Mr. Sutton walked across the lobby toward the dining room, the Great Dane got to his feet and started forward.

The next thing the family knew, Edgar Sutton was flat on his back on the floor, the Great Dane over him, and Mixed Blessing was pawing away at the leather bag, giving excited yips and yelps.

"Aha, sir! Stand aside!" Theodore cried, which hardly seemed necessary, for the man was flat on the floor.

"What in the blazes . . . ?" growled Mr. Sutton.

"This is the maniac bomber?" cried Mother.

"What?" said the man on the floor.

Joseph took hold of Mixed Blessing's collar, while Theodore cautioned the family to stand back. Then, gingerly—very, very gingerly—Father put out one hand to open the valise.

"Should the bomb go off when I open this, my dear," he said to Alma, "remember that my last words were, and always will be, 'I love you.'"

Mother dabbed at her eyes as Theodore opened the bag.

There inside were five different kinds of sausage, two of baloney, one of salami, and a half-dozen varieties of knockwurst.

"What is the meaning of this?" cried Edgar Sutton, picking himself up off the floor. "I am a respectable sausage salesman, and did not expect to be treated this way in a reputable hotel."

"My good man," said Theodore humbly, closing the leather bag again and helping brush off Mr. Sutton's pants. "I heartily apologize, but it was your safety that had my full concern." He explained about the maniac bomber, and how the Great Dane had been trained as a sniffer.

"I only wanted to assure our guests of their safety, and if you will allow us to treat you to dinner, sir, both your meal and your room will be on the house," Theodore said.

That seemed to make Mr. Sutton feel much better, and at last he agreed to let bygones be bygones, and Mother ushered him to the very best table by the window.

Was it possible, Bernie wondered, that in all this attention to canine sniffing, the real bomber was getting ready to strike again?

Fifteen

Stalking Steven

Weasel, however, had an idea.

"What we do," he told his friends, "is stalk Steven Carmichael."

"You really think he's the bomber?" asked Bernie.

"All I know is that both times a bomb's gone off, Delores's old boyfriend has been there. Whether he's setting them off or whether someone's after Steven, it just makes sense to trail him and see what happens. Everywhere he goes, we go. We don't let him out of our sight for a single minute."

"And if he gets on a bus to Fort Wayne to visit his floozie?" asked Georgene.

"Well, we'll follow him everywhere except on a bus, I guess," Weasel told her. "Do you know where he lives, Bernie?"

Bernie did, in the apartment house behind the library; and over they went.

Carmichael, it said on one of the mailboxes inside the door.

"Now what?" asked Bernie. "We sit on the steps and wait for him to come in or go out?"

"We hide in the bushes," said Weasel. "He doesn't own a car does he?"

"Not anymore," Bernie said. "I think Delores spent all his money."

"All the more reason for him to hate Middleburg," Georgene said.

They must have sat in the bushes for thirty minutes, and Bernie was sure he was being eaten by every bug alive.

Women went in carrying sacks of fruit, teenagers came out carrying boom boxes on their shoulders, young men came in to visit their friends, and old men came out to stand on the steps, scratch their stomachs, and go back inside.

At last Bernie heard the sound of more footsteps coming down the stairs of the apartment building. Through the glass doors he could see Steven Carmichael walking toward the door. Out he came, whistling to himself, and walked briskly down the sidewalk.

"Follow him!" Weasel whispered.

Bodies crouched low, the three friends scuttled along

in the bushes, colliding every so often and bumping heads, then hurrying on, bent over double so Steven could not see them.

When the bushes disappeared, however, Bernie and his friends had to follow some distance behind Steven, walking single file, ducking in doorways, hiding behind trees and trash cans.

Finally, at the drugstore on the next corner, Steven Carmichael went in.

"Aha!" said Georgene.

"Aha, what?" said Bernie. "You think he went to the drugstore to buy a bomb?"

"Drugstores have all kinds of things that explode," Georgene told him.

They peered in the window, but all they could see was Steven Carmichael with his back to them.

"What do you bet the drugstore blows up as soon as he leaves?" whispered Georgene.

It was a thought. An awful thought. But Bernie had still another idea.

"What if we aren't the only ones stalking Steven? What if somebody else is following him with a spyglass right this minute, and has a bomb waiting to go off as soon as Steven steps outside?" he whispered back.

Inside, Steven was paying for something at the cash register. The clerk handed him a brown paper bag. A large bag. A large, bulky, brown paper bag, and then Steven Carmichael was coming straight out the door, and it was all Bernie and his friends could do to make it to the alley before he passed.

"We've got to find out what's inside the bag," said Weasel. "This could be important."

"I say we trip him," said Bernie. "Let's hide in the bushes near the apartment building, and just as he turns up the walk, we poke out a big stick and trip him."

As they sprinted along from building to building, alley to alley, Bernie found a large branch beneath a tree, and he took it along.

They made it back to the bushes before they heard Steven whistling once again. Crouching, Bernie waited with Georgene and Weasel until Steven Carmichael was passing right on the other side, and silently he stuck the long branch straight out in front of the man with the bag. Down Steven went.

KA-POW!

There was an explosion, all right. Glass and fluid drained down all over Bernie, Georgene, and Weasel, and it wasn't until Bernie licked his lips that he tasted Coca-Cola. A sack full of six-packs lay strewn all over the sidewalk, and Steven Carmichael's clothes were drenched.

Bernie felt truly terrible.

"What happened?" asked Steven, his glasses sitting lopsided on his head.

Bernie, Georgene, and Weasel rose slowly up from behind the bushes.

"Are you all right?" asked Bernie.

"Can we dry you off?" asked Georgene.

Steven Carmichael was clearly shaken. It was as though he had survived two bombings, but this was the final straw. He kept blinking as Coca-Cola dripped off his eyebrows and eyelashes, and he didn't even try to get up. Bernie wondered if perhaps one of the Coke bottles had landed on Steven's head.

"Well, we won't leave until we know you're all right," said Weasel. "How about taking a little test? What's your last name?"

"Carmichael . . . I *think*," said the man. "I'm not sure of anything anymore."

"Have you ever fired a gun?" asked Weasel.

"A BB gun on occasion," said Steven.

"Do you like the Fourth of July?"

"My favorite holiday," Steven told him.

"One last question," said Weasel. "If Delores Magruder were the last woman on earth, would you marry her?"

"I would turn around and start running, and I wouldn't stop till I got to Australia," said Steven, getting to his feet and brushing off the seat of his pants.

"I think you are quite yourself now," Weasel told him.

Steven went back into his apartment building for a broom and dustpan.

Georgene turned to Weasel. "So what does any of *that* prove?"

"He knows how to fire a gun, he loves the Fourth of July, and Delores is the last woman on earth he'd ever marry," said Weasel. "Put them all together and you have . . . uh . . . ." Weasel stopped and scratched his head. "Well, I'm not sure. A man who would do anything to keep from marrying Delores."

"Even blow himself up?" asked Georgene. "We've had some stupid ideas, Weasel, but this was the dumbest one yet."

Sixteen

Man-to-Man

Bernie didn't know what to think. Mr. Fairchild seemed to feel that the bomber might strike the hotel, yet the only person Mixed Blessing had reacted to, besides the sausage salesman, was Joseph. And Joseph was the last person in the world whom Bernie wanted to be the bomber.

Of course, Mixed Blessing always reacted to Joseph. Joseph was the one, after all, who had brought him home to the hotel to live after the owner had decided he was too big to keep any longer, and had left him on the steps of the animal hospital.

Yet why would Joseph want to bomb the hotel where his dad was manager? The hotel the family had made their home?

There was no reason that Bernie could think of, yet he had to admit that his brother had been acting very strangely. The only thing left to do was to simply ask Joseph. Just come right out and ask him.

The incident with the sausage salesman, however, was all the family could talk about.

"Do you see what happens when we allow suspicions to overtake our reason?" Theodore said to his family. "If we put each of our guests through a sniff test, we shall wind up with no guests at all. I am thoroughly muddled."

"And if we let the bomber in this hotel, we shall wind up with no hotel at all," said Mother.

"Either way," said Delores, spearing a piece of broccoli, "we shall be out on the streets again, blown about the country like dry leaves in the wind."

"Or blown sky high," added Bernie darkly.

"I *like* it here!" Lester said. "I want to stay in Middleburg."

"And stay we shall," said Theodore, getting control of himself once again. "I have no intention of letting a maniac bomber chase us out of town. I have faith that any person with any civility at all will take one look at this hotel and know what a grand old building it was in its time, and how important it is that it *stay* that way."

"I agree," said Joseph. "Who would want to bomb a hotel?"

"But then who would want to bomb a bus depot?" Bernie argued.

"A bus depot is not a hotel, my boy, with a grand

staircase and thirty of the finest hotel rooms in Middleburg."

"Thirty of the *only* hotel rooms in Middleburg," added Delores dryly. "Because this is the only hotel there is."

Mother was still nervous. "I would feel much, much better, Theodore, if there was some way we could be sure there was no dynamite in the hotel. *Couldn't* we have Hildegarde take Mixed Blessing along with her when she cleans the rooms and sort of sniff around a bit?"

"If *you* were staying in a hotel, Alma, my precious little dove, would you want a dog coming into your room while you were out and sniffing through your belongings?" asked her husband. "You would not."

"Then we'll have to get used to the idea of being blown to bits and scattered about the country like *dust* in the wind," Delores declared.

Lester looked as though he were going to cry. Bernie didn't feel so good himself.

But Joseph just excused himself and left the table.

Bernie left, too. Joseph brushed his teeth and Bernie brushed his teeth. Joseph walked down the hall to the cellar stairs, Bernie following some distance behind.

By the time Bernie reached the wooden door at the bottom, however, he found it locked again. It would not budge.

Bernie decided not to knock. Instead, he put his ear right up against the door and listened.

Click . . .click . . . tick tock . . . swish swoosh. . . .

Chills ran up and down his spine. How *did* you make a bomb, anyway? At last he gave up listening and sat down on the stairs to wait. A half hour passed. An hour. An hour and twenty minutes.

Lewis, one of the cats, slunk down the stairs, sniffed at Bernie, and then, after being stroked from head to tail, went back up again. Then Clark, the other cat, came down and went to the wooden door. He meowed once or twice, wanting to use the litter box, then went upstairs also.

At last Mixed Blessing lumbered down and lay on the floor right outside the heavy wooden door.

Bernie leaned his head against the wall and his eyes began to close. He worried that he might actually fall asleep in the warmth of the stairway, when at last the door opened and Joseph came out, stepping across the Great Dane, and was startled when he saw Bernie.

"What are *you* doing down here?" he asked.

"Wanting to ask you the same question," Bernie replied. He ached when he said it. He loved his brother and could not bear to think of Joseph doing anything he shouldn't. "What are you doing down here alone so much, Joseph, that you won't tell anybody?"

Joseph didn't really look him in the eye as he started up the stairs. In fact, he looked as though he might walk right by his brother, but Bernie planted himself in the middle of the step so that Joseph couldn't pass at all.

"I live here, too, Bernie. Do I have to tell you everything I do?" Joseph asked.

"No, but you never had secrets before."

"I don't ask you what you're doing when *you* go off by yourself, do I?"

"No, but I'd tell you if you asked."

"Well, let's put it this way. When I finish what I'm doing, it will be in all the newspapers," Joseph said, and this time he stepped right over Bernie and went on up to the Magruder apartment.

Seventeen

The Letter M

"I hate to tell you this, Bernie," Officer Feeney said the next day when Bernie met him at the corner, "but I'm afraid your sister is our prime suspect. In *my* book, anyway. She's the only one I can think of who had a motive. The bus depot was bombed just two times, and each time Steven Carmichael was either coming or going. Now if that ain't two and two adding up to four, you don't know your arithmetic."

"What about Steven Carmichael bombing it himself?" Bernie asked.

"And him almost going up with the building?" asked Feeney. "Use your head. If *any*one looks guilty, Bernie, it's your sister."

"But where would Delores get any dynamite? She can't even make egg salad! How could she make a bomb?" said Bernie.

"Bernie, a woman scorned can do most anything."

"Okay. Arrest her."

"Well, that's just not the way it's done. People won't talk when they're being accused—the spotlight on them, so to speak. You have to approach it gently. A little kindness goes a long way."

"Hasn't the bomb squad come up with something? All this time and they haven't discovered anything?" Bernie asked, desperate now to save his sister, no matter what she'd done.

"Well, this is just between you and me and the lamppost," Feeney said, "but what *I've* heard—way of the grapevine, you know—is that somebody disguised the bomb like a package tied up with rope, then set it off from a distance." He pulled a piece of frayed cord from his pocket. "Take a good look, Bernie. Each time a bomb has gone off at the bus depot, they've found a piece of this. That's what tied the package, they figure."

Officer Feeney held the cord at each end and pulled slightly. "And you know what I'm thinking, Bernie? I'm thinking this might be the same kind of cord they use at the parachute factory where your sister works. Thought just came to me this morning, but I'm not turning this one over to the bomb squad. No siree. I'm saving this little thought under my own hat, and when I arrest your sister, maybe they'll take me off the Bessledorf beat at last, and put me on homicide where I belong."

Bernie didn't say anything. *Couldn't* say anything, because not only could that cord have come from the parachute factory, as Feeney said, but it could have come from the veterinary college as well—the kind of cord they used for a leash when they had to take dogs from one part of the clinic to another.

He went swimming with Georgene and Weasel that afternoon because he thought he'd go nuts with worry. He wanted to forget the bombs, but that's all his friends could talk about.

"I'd guess the safest place to be in Middleburg right now is this swimming pool," Weasel said, floating around on his back. "Nobody's going to bomb a pool."

Without his glasses on, of course, Weasel couldn't see anything at all, and he kept bumping into other swimmers so often that Georgene finally went ahead of him to warn them away.

"I think Mr. Fairchild is right. Your hotel's probably next, Bernie," Georgene said. "The maniac might *know* that the police will be thick around the bus depot, so he'll look for something else to bomb. The hotel's right next door, so why not?"

"The funeral home is close by, too," Bernie told her. "Why couldn't that be bombed instead of us?"

"And have dead bodies all over the place?"

"They were *already* dead bodies. In the hotel, they'd be dead *live* bodies," said Bernie.

KA-POW!

There was a huge explosion of water at the far end of the pool, and Bernie almost jumped out of his skin. Georgene put her hands up over her head, and Weasel dived down under the surface.

But it was no bomb, just a two-hundred-pound kid trying a cannonball in the deep end. The lifeguard frowned.

"Boy, we're really nervous," said Georgene later as they dried off. "I've been jumping at every little thing lately. When you've got someone going around setting off bombs, and you don't know who it is or why he's doing it or where he's going to strike next, you feel like staying in bed with the covers over your head."

Weasel agreed. "I think they should round up all suspects—anyone the police even *think* might be suspects—and put them all in jail. Then, if the bombings stop, we'll know it was one of them, and all the police have to do is figure out which one."

"You can't do that!" Bernie protested. "If I didn't like somebody—you, for example—all I'd have to do is go to Officer Feeney and say, 'I think Weasel did it,' and you'd go to jail."

"Then *I'd* say that *you* did it, and we'd be even," said Weasel.

"And you'd both be in jail along with a hundred other people," Georgene told them. "There's got to be a better way."

Bernie agreed. So far they'd suspected a sausage salesman at the hotel, and if they started arresting anybody who *might* have bombed the bus depot, well . . . He almost wished he could say that Mrs. Buzzwell did it. The hotel would be a lot quieter if *she* wasn't around.

"I've got a plan," he said at last, and told them about the piece of rope Feeney had shown him. "I'm going to walk up to the parachute factory this afternoon when Delores gets off work and take a look at some parachute cord—see if it looks the same. And then I'm going to check on the rope they use at the veterinary college."

"Oh, Bernie," said Georgene sorrowfully. "It's just so awful. A convict in your family. A murderer, almost!"

"I know," said Bernie.

As it happened, it was Mrs. Buzzwell he encountered when he walked back inside that afternoon.

"Well, Bernie," she said, "is your father going to wait until we are all blown sky high, or is he going to do something about this bomber? The maniac could be in the room just below mine! He could be in the dining room with a bomb right under the table where I sit. He could be right here in the lobby where. . . ."

"Awk! Awk!" screeched Salt Water, and Mrs. Buzzwell jumped.

"We're keeping an eye on everybody who comes in," Bernie said, trying to be polite.

It didn't help that old Mr. Lamkin was watching a TV program called "The Bomb Squad," or that Felicity

Jones was over in a corner having a seance on a tea table all by herself, and when Bernie asked if she had any psychic information yet about the bomber, she said, "I know one of the bomber's initials so far. It's an M."

Bernie's heart seemed to sink right down to his knees, then his ankles, and finally he felt as though it were lodged somewhere between his toes.

It could, of course, stand for Miss, Mister, or Missus, and, knowing Felicity, Bernie thought, that was probably it. But it could also stand for Magruder, and that could mean either Delores or Joseph. He found himself going back to his original suspicion: maybe Delores had asked Joseph to make the bomb for her and to set it off.

Theodore was standing outside the hotel, hosing down the sidewalk. Bernie went out to talk to him.

"Dad, if a sister and a brother both go to jail, can they stay in the same cell?" he asked.

"I think not, my boy."

"Could they stay in side-by-side cells?"

"No. Women would be in a prison all their own."

"They couldn't even see each other?"

"Not until they'd served their time."

Bernie sat down on the curb, feeling sad.

"Bernie," said his father, "whatever you've done, it can't possibly be that bad." He came over and looked down at Bernie. "What *did* you do?"

"Nothing at all," Bernie told him. "Honest."

▲▼▲

At five of five, Bernie walked up the steep hill to the parachute factory and waited for his sister. Promptly at five o'clock, the whistle blew, the doors opened, and out poured a gaggle of women who spent their days sewing straps and pounding grommets on parachutes.

"Bernie!" said Delores. "What are you doing here?"

"I just thought I'd walk home with you," Bernie told her. "Do me a favor, Delores. Could you get me a little piece of parachute cord? The rip cord, maybe? I want to make something."

"You're asking me to steal?"

"No. I just need a scrap. Something from the waste bin."

"We have all different sizes of ropes and cords. What size do you want?" Delores asked.

"Oh, maybe about this big," Bernie said, crooking his finger to demonstrate.

"Well, come on in and look for yourself," Delores said, taking him back inside, where he was almost run over by all the women coming out.

Once inside, however, Bernie stared, for the floor was covered with bits and pieces of string, rope, cloth, grommets, and cord of all sizes and shapes.

Bernie took three or four different pieces, as close as he could get to the size Officer Feeney had shown him, and put them in his pocket. Then he set off down the hill with his sister, and decided to give Delores a little test of his own.

"Delores," he said, "if there was only one man on the face of the earth, and he was Steven Carmichael, what would you do?"

"Is that a trick question?" she asked. "Give him a good hard jab to the chin! What else?"

"Well, just answer one more," said Bernie. "If you could be a famous movie star or a demolition expert, which would you choose?"

"A movie star who can't eat anything but lettuce? No thank you," said Delores. "I'd choose demolition expert any day."

Eighteen

The Gentle Approach

The next evening the family was just having dessert —chocolate cream pie—when Officer Feeney showed up at the back door to the apartment once again.

"Does that guy always have to appear at mealtime?" Delores complained.

"Why, dear, he will be there at mealtime for the rest of your life," said Mother.

"He *what?*" Delores demanded.

Mother looked chagrined. "Well . . . uh . . . what I mean is . . . it's rather nice, don't you think, to have a policeman look after you . . . I mean, *in* on you?"

Bernie let Officer Feeney in, and the policeman politely took off his cap.

"Just looking in on you again, ma'am," he said, as though to Mother, but his eyes were on Delores.

"With a fork in hand, no doubt," Delores mumbled.

"Excuse me?" said Feeney.

"She said to take a fork and join in," Theodore said hastily.

"Don't mind if I do," said Feeney.

Mother pulled out a chair. "Sit down! Sit down! Why, Hiram, you're like a member of the family."

"Thank you!" said Feeney. And when an extra-large piece of pie had been set before him, the piece that Bernie had been hoping to get, the officer looked across the table at Delores. "And how are things going for Delores here?"

"Same as always," Delores said, lifting her fork to her lips and taking a bite of pie.

"But what I want to know, Delores, is how are things going in your personal life?" Feeney continued. "The men, you know. . . ."

"*What* men?" Delores snapped. "Every man I've met so far, Feeney, has been a rotten rat. Love me and leave me, that's the truth. If I had a dollar for every man who's jilted me, I'd buy a stick of dynamite and blow 'em to kingdom come, don't think I wouldn't."

Bernie could hardly breathe. Feeney paused, his fork halfway to his mouth.

"Now, Delores," said Mother, clucking her tongue.

Feeney put down his fork and tucked his napkin under his chin. "Surely you don't mean that. Blow up a building just to get back at a man who did you wrong?"

"Who said anything about blowing up a building,

Feeney? It's the man I'm talking about, wher*ever* he was. He always gets away with it, though. I always get the short end of the stick. What I'd like to do is get 'em *all* in a room together, *then* let it blow. Bam!"

"Delores, my dear," said her mother, "I'm sure that Hiram would like to see your cheerful, generous, sweet, and kindly side for a change. What man wants to listen to a woman carry on like this?"

"Oh, no, no, no, Mrs. Magruder," said Feeney. "Let her talk. Let her get it off her chest."

"Don't you go talking about my chest, Feeney, and keep your eyes on your pie," Delores warned.

Feeney took another big bite. "Tell you what. After dinner, why don't you and I take a little stroll down the alley and talk things over. Okay with you, Delores?"

"A little walk down the *alley?*" Delores cried.

"The alley—the sidewalk—the park, wherever. It will do you good."

"Indeed it will, my girl, and I want you to go," said Theodore, with authority. "As soon as you have finished dessert and brushed your teeth, you will go for a walk with Hiram."

"Is that an order?" asked Delores.

"You may consider it so," said her father.

With a heavy sigh, Delores got up from the table and went to brush her teeth. As soon as she and Officer Feeney had gone out the back door, Mother smiled triumphantly around the table.

"Well, my dears," she said, "you might as well get used to the idea that Hiram Ignatious Feeney is going to be your brother-in-law."

Joseph suddenly looked up from his pie. "What?"

"Now don't breathe a word of it," Mother said. "Not even to Delores. Every bride wants to think that nobody else knows her little secret, so when the time is right, she will announce the engagement herself."

"To *Feeney?*" Joseph was still staring. Bernie wasn't sure, but he wondered if Joseph weren't looking a little pale.

"Why *not* Feeney?" asked Father.

"Why *not* have a policeman around to look after things?" asked Mother.

"Yeah," said Bernie, studying his brother closely. "We don't have anything to hide."

Joseph excused himself from the table, and the last Bernie saw of him, he was disappearing down the cellar steps.

When Delores came back a half hour later, she was in an even worse mood than when she left.

"That Feeney!" she complained. "All he did was ask questions. Was I dating anyone else right now? he wants to know. How long did I hold a grudge? What was most important to me—my own happiness or making Steven Carmichael miserable?"

Mrs. Magruder just smiled. "And what did you answer, my dear?"

"Of course I'm not dating anyone right now; I can hold a grudge forever; and the one thing that would make me happiest of all would be to make Steven Carmichael as miserable as possible," said Delores, and flounced down the hall to her room.

"Just the type of questions a man asks a woman to help him capture her heart," Mrs. Magruder murmured, still smiling.

Nineteen

Checking Joseph Out

"As soon as I can get Feeney off to myself," Bernie said to his friends the next day at the pool, "I'm going to check those pieces of cord from the parachute factory with the piece he got from the bomb squad. If none of them match, maybe Delores won't be a suspect anymore."

The three friends had given up trying to make the world record in coasting the farthest on a skateboard, and were practicing to see who could stay under water the longest. So far they hadn't stayed very long.

"And while we're waiting for you to see Feeney," Georgene said, "I have another idea."

She pulled herself up on the edge of the pool and sat dangling her feet in the water. "If Delores *is* making the bombs, she had to learn how. And if she came right out and *asked* someone, he'd probably turn her in to the police. So I figure she got a book from the library."

"The *library!*" exclaimed Bernie.

"Do you think you can just walk in a library and get a book on blowing up a bus depot?" asked Weasel.

"No, but you could get a book called *Dynamite: Its History and Uses* or *Blast Your Own Quarry* or something," Georgene told them.

"I don't know," said Bernie. "Even if there *is* a book by that name, the librarian won't tell you who's checked it out. That's confidential."

"Oh," said Georgene. "*Big* problem!" They crawled out of the water and lay on their stomachs in the sun while smaller children leaped across them.

"*I've* got it!" Weasel said suddenly, raising his head. "Go to the library, Bernie, and tell them your sister thinks she has a book overdue but can't remember the name of it and wants to know what she should be looking for."

"It's worth a try," Georgene said.

So when they were through swimming and had dressed again, they got on their bikes and rode to the library. A blond librarian with bright red lipstick looked down at them from behind the desk.

"Excuse me," said Bernie, "but my sister Delores thinks she might have a book overdue but can't remember what she checked out last. Can you help?"

"Why, Bernie, your sister hasn't checked out a book in the last year," the librarian told him. "If Delores

Magruder ever walked in this library and asked for a book, I'd fall over backward in a dead faint."

"Oh . . . uh . . . I meant my *brother*!" Bernie said hastily. "My *brother*, of course! Joseph!"

"Oh, Joseph. He *is* a bit forgetful, isn't he?" the librarian said. "Well, let me see if I can help."

The librarian pressed some buttons on her computer and found Joseph's name. "As a matter of fact, he *does* have one overdue: *How to Start Your Own Corporation and Cut the Competition*. That's the title."

A bus depot? Joseph was starting his own bus depot, and was trying to bomb his competitor out of business? Bernie wondered.

"A lot of good that does us," said Georgene, when they were outside again.

"It does a *lot* of good," said Bernie, but he wasn't at all happy about it. And he told them how it was no longer Delores he suspected but Joseph.

"Joseph!" said Weasel, sitting right down on the curb. "Joseph?"

"I'm afraid so," said Bernie. "I've never seen him act this way before," and he told them all he had seen.

The three friends were quiet for a long while.

"Well, now that you mention it, maybe it isn't so surprising that it's Joseph," said Georgene. "He always was a little strange, Bernie. You know that."

"I *don't* know that," said Bernie, bristling. "He's been my favorite person in the whole family."

"But remember the time he carried a bowl of guppies

99

around in his car, and when he came to pick you up at school, you had to hold the bowl between your knees?" said Weasel.

How else would you get guppies home without spilling them? Bernie wondered.

"And the time he tried to psychoanalyze Salt Water because the bird kept saying 'Drop dead'?"

That seemed natural, too.

But then Bernie thought about the time Joseph got up in the night to give a parakeet shots, and the way he rubbed his hand over Lewis and Clark every morning, and the way he used Mixed Blessing as a foot warmer in cold weather. *Was* Bernie's older brother a little strange?

As Mother was putting towels away in the linen closet that afternoon, Bernie folded each one and handed it to her to be helpful.

"Mom," he said, "did you notice anything strange about Joseph after he was born?"

"Joseph? Well, let's see. His first word was 'Bang.' I remember that."

"Did he . . . did he ever hurt things? Pull the wings off butterflies or anything?"

"Joseph? Of course not."

"Did he ever get into trouble with the neighbors?"

"He ate Mrs. Logan's petunias once when we lived in Kansas."

"But did any teachers ever tell you he was weird?"

"Bernie, why are you asking these awful questions? Of course not!"

"Just taking a little family history," Bernie said.

When Joseph came home later, Bernie asked, "Do you think you could get me a piece of rope from the veterinary college, Joseph? The kind you use as a leash for dogs?"

"Sure. How big a piece do you want?"

"Oh, just any little piece will do. A foot of it, maybe?"

"I'll try to remember," Joseph said and, as usual, went right down to the cellar and locked the door.

Twenty

The Wedding Party

Bernie had never seen his parents so excited.

"Once we have a policeman in our family, we'll *never* have to worry about bombs," Theodore said to his wife when Bernie was listening. "It will be like our own security guard, Alma. Even when he's not on duty, he'll keep an eye on the Bessledorf because he'll know his beloved is sleeping peacefully inside."

Mother and Father were going over bills at the kitchen table in the apartment, and Bernie was sitting quietly on the back steps, with Lewis in his lap and Clark waiting a turn.

"What I have to do," said Bernie's mother, "is draw up the plans for the wedding, so that when Delores announces her engagement, we at least have something to start with. I wonder if Officer Feeney has a brother. If not, Joseph could be best man, don't you think? Bernie could be an usher, and Lester could be the ring bearer."

"My dear, isn't Lester a little old for ring bearer?" asked Theodore.

"It's not my fault that Feeney didn't propose earlier," Mother told him. "Now, Wilbur Wilkins plays the trumpet, you know. Perhaps we could use him somehow."

"Why, Alma, you're not thinking of hiring a handyman to play for our daughter's wedding, are you?"

"Only a few notes when Delores gets ready to descend the grand staircase. Once the ceremony is over, I thought we might hold the reception in the hotel dining room, with Hildegarde presiding over the guest book."

There was another voice in the kitchen now as Joseph came home from work. "Wedding plans already, Mom? Why don't you make a circus out of it while you're at it?" he said. "Felicity Jones could hold seances off in one corner, Mrs. Buzzwell could direct traffic, and Mr. Lamkin could check the coats."

"Now don't you get snippity, Joseph," Mother told him. "Your sister marrying Feeney could be the best thing that ever happened to her."

"So she can sleep until noon and watch the afternoon soaps?" said Joseph. "I just don't see her and Feeney making a good match, and it's time somebody said so."

"Well, that is for them to decide, not us," declared Theodore.

"Then we should let them decide it, and not sit around planning a wedding before they're even engaged," Joseph said.

"I would think you'd be happy for your sister," sulked Mother.

"I tell you what," said Joseph. "If Feeney pops the question, my little combo, 'The Cat's Pajamas,' will play at the reception for free."

Lester came into the kitchen then, because Bernie heard his voice next: "If Delores marries Feeney, can I choose the cake?"

"Indeed you cannot, that's up to the bride," said Mother. "But for you, I will suggest that at least one of the layers be chocolate with little frosted flowers on the side."

And then it was Delores coming up the back walk after still another stroll with Officer Feeney. Bernie followed them in.

"Delores!" said Lester, when he saw his sister. "Mom says one layer of the wedding cake will be chocolate."

"What wedding cake? Who's getting married?" asked Delores.

"Why, I'm sworn to secrecy," Mother said, a twinkle in her eye. "All I can tell you is it's someone in this hotel."

"Don't tell me it's Felicity Jones!" Delores cried. "If Felicity Jones gets married before I do, Mother, I shall go to the top of the courthouse and jump off."

"Bungee jumping?" Lester cried.

"Now dear, don't talk that way. Of course it's not Felicity. You'll know when the time comes, I can promise you that."

"Will I be invited?" Delores asked, still curious.

Mr. and Mrs. Magruder laughed, while Feeney merely looked puzzled.

"Of *course* you'll be invited," said her father. "Now not a word more about this, *any*body!" And he glared at Lester in particular.

Bernie followed Joseph down the hall to his older brother's bedroom.

"Joseph," he said, "I was at the library tonight, and the librarian mentioned that you have a book overdue."

"Son of a gun!" said Joseph. "I forgot all about it."

"Joseph, what kind of a company are you starting, and why do you have to cut the competition?" Bernie pleaded. "Listen. I don't know why you're doing what you are, but somebody's going to get hurt."

Joseph stared at him for a moment. "Bernie, in the business world, somebody *always* gets hurt. If you can't stand the heat, get out of the kitchen."

"What?" asked Bernie.

"Mind your own business," said Joseph.

Twenty-one

Double Fudge

Bernie knew what would happen if he told his parents what he suspected.

"Joseph?" they would say. "Our first-born son? A bomber? Are you out of your mind?"

It was Joseph who was possibly out of his mind. Joseph who might be a kind veterinarian student by day and a maniac bomber at night. What if the next bomb that went off actually killed somebody? Wouldn't Bernie be partly responsible for not having told anyone about his suspicions? And why, although Joseph promised, did he keep forgetting to bring home any rope from the veterinary college? Did he know that Bernie suspected something?

Bernie had been taught to be honest and kind to his fellowman, and if people were in danger of being blown off the face of the earth and Bernie might have done something about it, was that being kind? So Bernie went to see Officer Feeney.

Actually, he knew that when Feeney was working his eight to four shift, he always stopped at the Sweet Shop when he got off duty and ordered a double fudge pecan sundae with whipped cream on top. And Bernie figured that the best time to ask a man *any*thing was when he had a double fudge pecan sundae with whipped cream in his belly.

So when Officer Feeney slid into his usual booth in the Sweet Shop with a spoon in one hand and his sundae in the other, Bernie got a glass of water at the counter and carried it over to the booth. He slid in across from Feeney.

"Too late, Bernie, I already ate the cherry," the policeman said.

"That's okay," said Bernie, and took a sip of water.

"And if you figure I'm giving you any of this whipped cream, you're wrong."

"It's all yours," said Bernie, but the double fudge ice cream *did* make him hungry.

"Then what are you hangin' around for?" asked Feeney.

"I wondered if you still had that piece of rope you showed me the other day that you got from the bomb squad?"

"Well, let me see, now. Maybe I do and maybe I don't," Feeney said, searching his pockets. "Aha! Here we go." He laid it out on the table. "You want it, you can have it. We've got more."

Slowly Bernie pulled out the three pieces of cord he had taken off the floor of the parachute factory. He put them on the table beside Feeney's, all in a row.

"What have you got there?" asked the policeman.

"Cord off the floor of the parachute factory," Bernie said, as he leaned forward to study them closely. And then he gave a sigh of relief.

"See, Feeney? They don't match. Almost, but not quite. Delores didn't do it after all." He swept all the pieces up in his hand and stuffed them in his pocket.

"Now that don't take her off the hook, Bernie. Maybe there's other cord around the factory you didn't see. Maybe she got rope from somewhere else. You're on the right track, though. This just means we've got more checking to do. Old Feeney's going to crack this case before the bomb squad does, I'll wager."

"I don't think you need to check anymore," Bernie said, in a small sad voice. "Because I think . . . I'm afraid . . . I know . . . who's setting off those bombs."

The spoon dropped out of Feeney's hand, and he leaned forward, his eyes as big as walnuts. "Who?" he mouthed, without making a sound.

"Joseph," said Bernie, feeling awful.

"What?" Feeney stared. "Joseph? Your brother? The veterinarian-to-be?" He seemed totally surprised, but not surprised enough to turn his ice cream over to Bernie. In fact, he took an even bigger bite, and licked the front and back of the spoon after he'd swallowed.

Bernie told him all the reasons he suspected Joseph.

"Well now, Bernie, just because a man goes down in his basement and wants a little privacy doesn't mean he's making bombs, you know."

"Yes, but why now, when somebody's bombing the bus depot? And if he's doing something legal, why can't he tell me?"

"Have you asked him?"

Bernie nodded soberly, as he watched the ice cream disappearing from Officer Feeney's bowl.

"What does he say?"

"None of your business."

"What?" Officer Feeney frowned.

"I mean, that's what Joseph says: 'It's none of your business.'"

"So what do you want *me* to do?"

"I want you to go down in the basement sometime when he's there and see what he's doing. You could also search his room."

"Bernie, Bernie, I can't do that! I can't just force my way into your brother's room or your basement without a search warrant."

"You can't?"

"No. It's in the Constitution."

Bernie sighed. "Well, *get* a search warrant then."

"There has to be *cause*. I have to give a good reason. Joseph has to be a prime suspect, and right off the bat, I'd say he isn't much of a suspect at all. What's the motive? But *Delores*, now—Delores has *every* reason in the world. Delores is so mad at Steven Carmichael she'd light the fuse herself, and I happen to think that's exactly what she did."

"But you're not getting anywhere with Delores. The cords don't match! She's not telling you anything. And meanwhile, the bomber could strike again." And suddenly Bernie had another idea. "Listen, Feeney. Joseph wants to start a business. I don't know what kind of business, but he wants to start his own corporation and cut the competition."

"How do you know that?"

"A book he got from the library. He hardly has any money, though, and won't until he gets through college. Since Delores has a job, and Delores has a motive, maybe Joseph is making the bombs for Delores and she's paying him a lot."

"Well," said the patrolman, "one of these days your sister is going to sing, Bernie. And when she does . . ." Feeney sighed. "I'm afraid she's going to get ten years. And if Joseph's in on it, he'll get the same."

Bernie swallowed.

Officer Feeney slid the rest of his sundae over toward Bernie just then, but it was only a gray mess in the bottom of the dish, and Bernie shook his head.

"I think I'll go home," he said, and left the Sweet Shop.

That evening when Weasel and Georgene came over again and noticed Joseph heading for the cellar, Bernie and his friends went outside and around to the frosted window of the basement.

"There's more than one way to skin a cat," said Bernie.

"To do *what?*" cried Georgene.

"See in the basement," said Bernie. "I don't care if Joseph *does* hear us. The last time I was down there, I unlocked one of the basement windows so that we could push it open from the outside. It hasn't been opened for years, and it's probably painted shut, but let's each put a hand on it, and when I say, 'One, two, three, push,' we'll all push together. The window will open, and we'll see what Joseph is doing before he can hide anything."

They all put their hands on the window. "One, two, three . . . push!" said Bernie.

They all pushed, the window fell open, and a burglar alarm went off.

Twenty-two

Smoke

Bernie, Georgene, and Weasel saw almost nothing in the basement because everything began happening at once.

As soon as the window fell open, a burglar alarm went off.

When the alarm went off, Mixed Blessing began to howl.

When the dog began to howl, the cats meowed, Salt Water squawked, Father and Mother came running, and all the residents ran to the door to look out.

Bernie and his friends were just picking themselves up off the ground when Mr. Magruder came rushing around the corner of the building.

"Where's the burglar?" he called out.

"I'll bop him myself!" cried Wilbur Wilkins, following close behind with a baseball bat.

"It's only us," said Georgene.

"We sort of lost our balance," said Weasel.

"Sort of pushed against the window," Georgene added.

"I guess we sort of fell in," Bernie told his father.

Theodore looked much relieved. "Well, it's an ill wind that blows no good, a dark night that brings no day, and a cold rain that grows no grass."

"Huh?" said Georgene and Weasel.

"If you hadn't fallen into the window, we would not have known whether the alarm would go off when we really needed it. Now that you have tested it for us, our guests have every reason to feel safe in our hotel."

"What's the commotion?"

Everyone turned to see Joseph's head at the basement window. "Anything wrong?"

"Just testing out the burglar alarm," said Mr. Magruder. "Lock that window if you please, Joseph. Thank you very much."

Joseph pushed the window closed again and disappeared from view.

"Are you ever going to find out what he's doing down there?" Bernie asked his father.

"Who down where?"

"Joseph. In the cellar."

"Bernie, my boy, that was *our* Joseph, in *our* cellar, so why should I ask what a man is doing in his very own home? When I see you in the kitchen or bathroom, do I

113

ask what you are doing? No, I do not." And with that, he and Wilbur Wilkins went back inside.

"So what did you see in the basement?" Bernie asked Weasel quickly.

"Nothing," said Weasel. "Georgene was in the way."

"What did *you* see?" Bernie asked Georgene.

"Nothing," she answered. "When the window opened, you bumped me, Bernie, and I scraped my knee. What did *you* see?"

"Nothing," Bernie said in disappointment. "Just the usual stuff. Absolutely nothing out of the ordinary at all."

They walked around in back to see if Mrs. Verona might have made some fresh cookies that day, when suddenly,

BOOM!

The ground shook beneath their feet, and the air was filled with smoke.

Bernie, Georgene, and Weasel stared at one another in horror, and then at the column of smoke that was rising up over the roof of the hotel.

They ran around to the front. Bernie sucked in his breath, for the canopy over the entrance had been blown to bits, the glass in the windows was broken, and the door was gone.

Mr. and Mrs. Magruder stood at the registration desk in shock, staring at the mess. The animals were carrying on something terrible. Mrs. Buzzwell was on the phone to the police, Felicity Jones was standing with her hands over her mouth, and old Mr. Lamkin was still trying to watch his favorite soap opera, "No Tomorrow," and simply turned the volume up.

There was a wail of sirens, and in moments a squad car pulled up. Officer Feeney was already running down the street, even though he was off duty, and soon there were reporters and photographers and policemen swarming all over the place.

Bernie began to feel sick inside. Somebody in his family could have been seriously hurt. Somebody in his family could have been seriously killed! His eyes opened wide when he saw Steven Carmichael standing there talking to Officer Feeney.

"I had just walked by the hotel about three minutes before the bomb went off," he was saying. "I could have been killed! This bombing has got to stop!"

And Joseph, who had appeared from out of the basement, said to Mr. Magruder, "Dad, this is getting serious! We've got a maniac bomber on the loose for sure!"

But most of all, Bernie was troubled because when Delores waltzed in five minutes later, she didn't seem that much surprised at all.

"If they don't find that bomber soon, we will all be buried in boxes," she said. "Mom, do we have anything cold to drink?"

Officer Feeney walked over to her side. "Delores, my dear," he said gently. "Does it surprise you to know that

Steven Carmichael walked by the hotel only minutes before the bomb went off?"

"It doesn't surprise me *what* Mr. Carmichael does, one way or another," said Delores. "I can only say that it was an unfortunate set of circumstances that Mr. Carmichael did not walk under the canopy a minute or two sooner. That would have made me a happy woman indeed."

Officer Feeney looked at Bernie, and Bernie gulped. The only *worse* thing that could happen did. The phone rang, and it was Mr. Fairchild.

"Okay, Magruder," he said. "I just heard the news. What's with this bomb business? You haven't made any enemies in Middleburg, have you? Who in blazes would want to bomb the canopy off the front of my hotel?"

Bernie could hear his yelling loud and clear.

"I . . . I don't know, sir," said Theodore. "I don't know who would be crazy enough to do something like that."

Delores climbed over the rubble there on the floor, went back to the apartment, and returned to lean against the registration desk, taking a long, long sip of ginger ale.

So who was it? Delores, who didn't seem to care? Joseph, who wouldn't tell what he was doing in the basement? Steven Carmichael, who seemed to have been present at every bombing? Or someone else that they hadn't even thought of yet?

Twenty-three

Joseph or Delores?

"Well," said Mother to Theodore on Saturday, after the carpenters had put on a new door, the glazier had put in new windows, the painter had repainted the lobby, and the fabricator had put on a new canopy. "I, for one, will feel much better when Delores and Officer Feeney are safely married and we have a police officer living under our roof."

Bernie, who was combing the cats, listened.

"So will I, my dear," said Father.

"But I must say, he is taking his own sweet time about proposing," Mother went on. "I just can't understand it. I can see the way he looks at her—he watches every move she makes, clings to every word, and he is so *gentle*, Theodore, and so kind to her, the way he looks deep into her eyes. If that's not love . . ."

"Patience, my dear. The course of true love never did

run smooth, and there's more than one way to cook a goose. He'll pop the question by and by."

"Do you remember when you proposed to me?" asked Mother, smiling shyly.

"Indeed I do, my dear. We were in a canoe. . . ."

"A rowboat," said Mother.

"And the moon was shining. . . ."

"It was midafternoon," Mother told him.

"And you had on the prettiest hat I have ever seen. . . ."

"I didn't have on any hat at all, Theodore."

"And when I popped the question, you said, 'I thought you'd never ask.'"

"Theodore, I did not. I said I'd have to think about it," Mother said, and she wasn't smiling anymore.

"Oh, my dear, let us not quibble over words. The fact is that we have loved each other all these years, and given the world four wonderful children, and living here in this grand hotel is the zenith of our lives. The peak, the top, the summit, the pinnacle, the . . ."

"I understand, my dear," said Mother. "Let's not go overboard."

When Bernie passed Delores's room later, he saw her playing darts, and he stopped and stared. He had never seen his sister playing anything in her life, because Delores did not play. Delores complained, argued, obstructed, and obfuscated, but she did not play. There she was, however, aiming a dart at her closet door. And there, on her closet door, was a picture of Steven Carmichael. She got him right on the nose.

"Delores," said Bernie. "I don't think I would do that if I were you."

"And why not?" asked Delores. "This is the man who jilted me, Bernie. This is the man who was going to give me a diamond ring, buy me a house, and cherish me as long as we both shall live, and what did he do? Proposed to a floozie from Fort Wayne."

"Did he really promise you all that?" asked Bernie.

"When a man kisses you good night, Bernie, what *else* could he mean?" asked Delores.

"Well . . . maybe he just liked the floozie better," Bernie said, trying to be reasonable.

Delores did not appreciate "reasonable."

"*Liked* her better?" she shrieked. "*Liked* her better? After promising me a diamond ring?"

"He didn't actually, you know," said Bernie, still hoping to win his case.

"He said I had beautiful fingers!" said Delores. "A man does not notice your fingers unless he plans to put something on them."

"But he didn't actually say the word 'marry,' did he?"

"He said he would like a house in the country, and a man does not say 'house' to a woman unless he plans to make her his wife."

"But did he *love* you?" Bernie decided to ask the sixty-four-thousand-dollar question.

"Bernie," said Delores, "how could he *not* love this face? These hands? These lips? This body? Steven Carmichael could have had it all, and he let me get away!" And she threw another dart that caught Steven just above one eye.

As Bernie went on down the hall to his room, he passed Joseph who was carrying a large bag in his arms. Joseph held the top tightly closed.

"Did you bring me the piece of rope I wanted?" Bernie asked.

"Why yes, as a matter of fact I did," Joseph said. "Look in my left pants pocket."

Bernie thrust his hand in Joseph's pocket and found the rope. It was a thin piece of cord—thinner, Bernie was sure, than the one Feeney had given him.

"Thanks," Bernie said, stuffing it in his own pocket with the others. And then, "What's in the bag?"

"Don't ask," said Joseph, and headed for the cellar stairs.

"Joseph," Bernie called after him, "what are you *doing* down there?"

"It's my business, Bernie. You'll find out soon enough," said Joseph.

Bernie went straight out the back door where Lester was trying to pump air in his bike tires and eat a jelly sandwich, both at the same time.

"Lester," said Bernie, "don't ever do anything illegal."

"What?" said Lester.

"One member of the family in jail at a time is enough," Bernie told him.

Back on the wall by the alley, Bernie took out all the cords from his pocket and laid them in a row. He studied each one. Every one was different from the others. The one he had got from Officer Feeney, however, was the most unusual-looking of all. Bernie couldn't quite figure out how, but it wasn't your ordinary piece of rope, of that he was sure.

He put the cords back in his pocket and went to get Georgene and Weasel. He wanted to get away. He wanted to forget the maniac bomber for a while, and soon the three friends were on their way to the pool.

"Look at it this way, Bernie," Georgene said. "If Delores goes to prison, you'll get her room. If Joseph goes to prison, you'll get his room. One way or another, you get a room of your own."

"Georgene!" Bernie was surprised at her. "There are more important things to think about than a room."

"You'll get an extra pork chop at dinner, too," said Weasel. "You'll get the extra piece of pie."

"There are more important things than pork chops and pie," Bernie declared. "Don't you understand that whatever Joseph's doing, and however awful Delores can be, they're still family, and I don't want anything bad to happen to them? Not to mention that Dad will be fired."

"I understand, Bernie," Georgene said softly. "I was just trying to make you feel better."

"Me, too," said Weasel. "No one wants a jailbird for a brother."

They paid admission to the pool, and all three ran to the water's edge and dived in.

The water was cool and comforting. It was like having somebody rub your belly and your back, both at the same time. Bernie wished he could stay in the pool for the rest of his life. He wished that he could just float around forever, watching the clouds, feeling the breeze on his face, and hearing the happy sounds of swimmers around him. He and his friends were just starting a race to the deep end, when:

KA-BOOM!

A water spout twenty feet high shot up through the air, and the diving board with it.

Twenty-four

Delores and Feeney

The only good thing about it was that nobody was hurt. The lifeguard was bruised a little when the diving board came down and grazed his elbow, but at the particular moment Bernie, Georgene, and Weasel had decided to race to the deep end, it was because nobody else happened to be down there.

Feeney, of course, was on the scene in less than five minutes. The bomb squad was also there, taking pictures of the diving board and the hole in the deep end where the water was rapidly disappearing. By the time the bomb squad got through with its investigation, the pool was as dry as a rock in the sun. Bernie and his friends hurriedly dressed for home, and were just leaving the pool area when Feeney came walking toward them.

"Well, Bernie," he said, "this is it. I'm afraid I'm going to have to arrest your sister."

"Why?" Bernie said, and could not believe that he felt tears in his eyes. It was the first time he could ever remember crying over Delores.

"Because," said Feeney, swinging his nightstick, "I just put in a call to Steven Carmichael. And it seems that Steven Carmichael, the very man to whom your sister thought she was engaged, was thinking about coming to the pool today, but decided to go shopping for a ring for his Fort Wayne beloved at the last moment."

"But, Feeney, it's a hot day!" Georgene protested. "A lot of people probably *thought* about coming to the pool. What does that prove?"

"True enough," said the policeman, "but consider this: whenever there's been a bombing, Steven Carmichael was either there, had just been there, was about to be there, or was considering going. Come on, Bernie, this was your idea, after all. Mr. Carmichael has no greater enemy in Middleburg than your sister, and you know it."

It seemed to Bernie that Officer Feeney was straining very, very hard to find the bomber. It seemed to Bernie that Feeney wanted so much to have his name in the newspaper as the officer who had found the culprit that he would arrest Delores on the slightest provocation.

But what was an eleven-year-old boy supposed to do when a big burly police officer suspected his sister? And if it *was* Delores who was planting bombs around Middleburg, then she should, of course, be brought to justice. He knew that as well as anybody.

"Could I . . . could I sort of warn her, so it won't be such a shock?" he asked the policeman.

"No, Bernie, I'm afraid that won't do. Delores might get it in her head to skip town, you know. Or worse yet, she might decide to plant one of those bombs on me."

It was one of the darkest days of Bernie's life. As the procession moved down the sidewalk—Officer Feeney in the lead with his nightstick, Bernie next, then Georgene, then Weasel—Bernie thought of the sadness this would bring his parents. If it were really Joseph doing the bombing instead of Delores, was he man enough to admit it, or would he let his sister go to jail and take the rap for him? Bernie knew that Officer Feeney was ready to make his case, for he even carried a folder of photographs of all the bombings.

As they entered the lobby of the hotel, Theodore looked up from the registration desk, Mother looked up from the plants she was watering over by the window, and Delores, who was sitting on the couch, her bare feet propped on the coffee table in the lobby, polishing her toenails, looked over at Feeney and yawned.

Old Mr. Lamkin, Felicity Jones, and Mrs. Buzzwell, however, went right on with their card game.

"Good afternoon, Feeney," said Father. "What was that noise we heard a half hour ago? Not another bomb, I hope?"

"I'm afraid so, Mr. Magruder," said Feeney. "Over at the pool."

"Oh, good heavens!" gasped Mother.

"No one was hurt, though, and things are under control," Feeney told her.

"Well, I guess we can be grateful for that," said Mother. "Will you sit awhile?"

Officer Feeney shook his head. "I must tell you that I am here on serious business."

Mother almost dropped the watering can and a smile spread across her face.

"Of course you are!" she said. "Please do sit down, Officer Feeney. Or may I call you Hiram now? Could we bring you some tea? A biscuit with strawberry jam, perhaps? That's your favorite, isn't it?"

"Ma'am, I do not want tea and I do not want biscuits. It is my sad duty to tell you that your beloved daughter Delores is under arrest."

"What?" Theodore thundered.

"What?" cried Mother. "Does this mean the wedding is off?"

"*What* wedding?" said Delores, leaning over to blow on her toenails.

"Oh, my darling, you and Officer Feeney were to be married right here in this hotel, and I had all the details planned, right down to the frosting on the cake," Mother sobbed.

"What?" cried Feeney and Delores together.

"I wouldn't marry him if he was the last lizard to crawl over the face of the earth!" Delores exclaimed.

"And beg pardon, ma'am," said Feeney, "but I wouldn't marry your daughter if you put a gun to my head. Delores, I arrest you on charges of planting bombs in the town of Middleburg."

"This is ridiculous!" said Theodore. "This is insane, Officer Feeney! Your mind has mottled, your wits have withered, your brain . . ."

"Eureka!" yelled Joseph, suddenly rushing up from the basement. "I did it! I did it! I have just invented the perfect exerciser for horses that have broken a leg. We don't have to shoot horses anymore when their legs are broken! With my home exerciser, the bones will heal and the horse will be as good as new."

"What?" cried Bernie, Georgene, and Weasel together.

"All this time I've managed to keep it secret while I was working on it, but now that it's ready to go, I'll start my own business! I'll be famous, Dad!" Joseph said.

But Mother was still weeping. "Joseph, how can you talk 'famous' when your very own sister is being carted off to the hoosegow?"

"What?" cried Joseph.

"Another bombing in Middleburg," said Father. "I didn't ever think that a child of mine would sink to such depths, and I still don't believe it, Feeney."

Over at the card table, the game had stopped.

"I shall move away from here at once," said Mrs. Buzzwell, getting to her feet.

"I would be much too afraid to stay in this hotel, with a maniac bomber in residence," said Felicity. "I will have to pack my bags."

"Well, if the two of you are leaving, I can't stay on by myself," said old Mr. Lamkin, and he rose to go as well.

"Why would Delores bomb Middleburg?" Joseph asked Officer Feeney.

"That's what I'd like to know," said Delores.

Feeney opened his folder and spread pictures of the bomb blasts out on the registration desk for all to see. The two bombs at the bus depot, the bombing of the hotel canopy, and he told them about the bombing that very afternoon at the swimming pool. Even Mrs. Buzzwell, Felicity Jones, and old Mr. Lamkin came over to look.

"In every one of these cases, Delores, your ex-boyfriend was present, going to be present, or was thinking about being present," he said. "What better way to wipe Steven Carmichael off the face of the earth than to bomb the daylights out of him."

"Do you think I would want to spend the rest of my life in jail while Steven Carmichael enjoys his floozy from Fort Wayne?" asked Delores. "Is your brain plain pickled?"

But Bernie was busy studying the photos. He looked at them very, very hard. And just as Officer Feeney was getting out the handcuffs to take Delores down to the station, he cried out, "Wait!"

Twenty-five

Caught!

"What is it?" asked Feeney.

"Look!" said Bernie, and pointed to one of the pictures.

Mr. and Mrs. Magruder, Georgene and Weasel, Officer Feeney, Joseph and Delores, and the hotel regulars all gathered around.

Bernie was pointing to the picture of a man in the crowd at the bus station.

"So?" said Feeney. "It's a man. So what?"

"I think he's the guy who did it," said Bernie.

"Why? Who is he?" asked Mother.

"I don't know," said Bernie.

They all stared at him as though he had just sprouted another head.

"Why do you think he's the bomber?" asked Feeney.

Bernie pointed to the other pictures as well. "Because

he's in *all* the pictures. Don't you think it's sort of strange that the same man would just happen to be in the crowd after each of the bombings?"

"Not a bit more peculiar than Steven Carmichael was, or had been, in each of the places Delores bombed," said Feeney.

"Now wait just a darn minute," said Delores.

"Besides, *you* were in all the crowd scenes, Bernie!" the policeman went on. "*I* was in all the crowd scenes. Maybe one of *us* did it!"

"Let me see the photo again, my boy," said Theodore.

Bernie chose the photo with the clearest picture of the man in it, and handed it to his father. Theodore got a magnifying glass from behind the registration desk and held it over the picture.

"I *know* that man!" he cried suddenly. "Mickey Scoates, I believe it is—the very same man who wanted to start a bungee-jumping business from the top of the court house."

"Who didn't get the permit," said Mother.

"Who stormed out of the room in a huff, if I remember!" said Father.

And then it all made sense. Bernie thrust his hand in his pocket and quickly pulled out the handful of cords Delores had given him from the parachute factory, the piece of rope Joseph had given him from the veterinary college, and the one he got from Officer Feeney. In front of his family, his friends, and the policeman, he took hold of the piece of rope from the bomb squad and pulled at it from both ends. It stretched twice as long and sprung back like a spring.

"A bungee cord!" cried Weasel and Georgene together. "Just like the one at the fair!"

"We'll put out an all-points bulletin," said Feeney, grabbing the phone at the registration desk and calling headquarters. "That man must be stopped." He quickly gathered up the photos to take to the police station.

"What about my invention?" asked Joseph.

"Later, Joseph, later," said his mother hurriedly.

"What about my wedding?" asked Delores.

"Wedding?" said Theodore. "My dear, you said that if Feeney was the last lizard to crawl over the face of the earth, you would not . . ."

"But if he's not going to arrest me, the least he can do is propose!" Delores wailed. "I deserve a *little* excitement!"

"Just how the ding dong did a wedding get mixed up in all this?" asked Feeney, but he now had other things on his mind. A crowd began to gather there in the hotel lobby, and someone said they had just seen the bungee man looking in the hotel window, then heading once again for the courthouse. Would he bomb the courthouse next?

When the bomb squad screeched to a stop in front of the hotel, Feeney ran out and jumped in, as much to get away from Delores as to catch the culprit, Bernie thought. He and Georgene and Weasel raced as fast as they could down the street and got to the courthouse almost as fast as the squad car.

The officers rushed into the building and up the stairs to the roof, Bernie and his friends close behind.

There was the man whose picture had appeared in all the photos.

"I don't care what you do to me, but I got even!" Mickey Scoates shouted as he backed closer and closer to the edge of the roof. "Why do some people get permits for business in Middleburg but not me? Why do some people get to run a bus depot, a hotel, and a swimming pool, but I don't get to run a bungee-jumping business?"

"Be careful," said Feeney. "You're about to fall off there."

But at that very moment the man's foot went off the edge of the building, and with his arms spread against the sky, he fell backward off the roof.

Bernie yelled, Georgene screamed, and Weasel hollered. They all rushed to the edge and looked over. There hung Mickey Scoates by one ankle, a bungee cord holding him about five feet from the ground.

"He's going to get away!" cried Georgene. "He's untying the cord around his ankle."

"We'll see about that," said Feeney, and he and the other policemen began pulling on the rope, hauling it up the side of the building until at last they had the bungee man in custody and took him off to the station.

"Well," said Bernie, as he and Georgene and Weasel walked back to the hotel. "The bungee man was just lucky that no one was killed in all those bombings, or he'd be going to jail for murder."

"So we don't have to worry about bombs when we walk down the street again," said Georgene. "Finally Middleburg is back to normal."

"Well, almost," said Bernie, as they walked into the lobby.

Because Delores was sitting at the registration desk writing a letter, and when Delores did anything besides paint her toenails or pluck her eyebrows, there was bound to be trouble. If Delores decided there wasn't enough adventure or romance in her life, she made up some herself.

"What do you suppose she's doing?" asked Weasel.

Bernie knew that the only way to find out was to wait quietly on the couch until something happened, so he sat on the sofa with Salt Water perched on his shoulder. Lewis lay in Georgene's lap, Clark in Weasel's, and Mixed Blessing slept at their feet.

Joseph came into the room carrying a large green trash bag filled to the brim in one hand, and a large green trash bag in the other hand.

"What's that?" asked Bernie.

"My invention," Joseph said glumly. "I just called my professor at the veterinary college to tell him what I'd done, and he says I'm too late. There's already a patent on a horse exerciser and by next year, new horse exercisers will be in production. Our college might even buy one."

"I'm really sorry, Joseph," Bernie said. "Even if you're never famous, you'll make a good vet anyway."

"Thanks, Bernie," said Joseph.

Mother came out into the lobby next, followed by Mr. Magruder, and they sat wearily down on the sofa across from Bernie and his friends.

"What a week! What a week!" said Father. "I hope Mr. Fairchild believes me when I tell him that the bungee jumper didn't have anything in particular against this hotel. He didn't care what he bombed, he was so bent on getting even."

"Oh, Mr. Fairchild will believe you, my dear. You're the best manager Mr. Fairchild has ever had, and he knows it," said Mother. "What I worry about is whether our dear Delores will ever recover from a broken heart."

"I will, and I have, Mother," said Delores, putting down her pen and walking over with a stamped and sealed letter, which she handed to Bernie.

"Mail this for me, will you?" she said. "It's a letter to Hiram Ignatius Feeney, and I can recite it by heart:

Dear Officer Feeney:
This is to inform you that I hereby reject your offer of marriage. You may beg, plead, entreat, and cajole,

but the answer now and forever will be no, no, a thousand times no. I only hope that you will recover from your broken heart, and will, as the years go by, stop lying awake at night, thinking of me. Live your life and let no mention of the name 'Delores' ever again escape your lips.

D.

"What?" cried Bernie.

"She's over it!" cried Mrs. Magruder delightedly. "Our darling daughter has recovered."

"An even better man than Officer Feeney will show up some day on our doorstep, my dear," said Theodore.

"Take it to the mailbox on the corner," Delores instructed Bernie. "The sooner it's on its way, the better."

"I'll drop it in the slot myself," he told her.

Bernie took the letter, and his two friends followed him outside. He knew that if he hadn't told Officer Feeney what he suspected about his sister, Officer Feeney would never have come calling. And if Feeney hadn't come calling, Mother would never have planned a wedding. And if Mother had never planned a wedding, Delores would never have got it in her head that she could count Feeney as one of her rejected suitors. Bernie had got Feeney into this, and it was up to him to get him out.

"I can't believe she wrote that," said Georgene, as they walked slowly down the sidewalk.

"Are you really going to mail it?" asked Weasel.

"Of course," said Bernie. When they reached the corner, he walked right past the mailbox, out into the middle of the street, and dropped the letter through a slot in the manhole cover, down to the sewer below.

F
NAY

Naylor, Phyllis
Reynolds

The bomb in the
Bessledorf bus